MISSING

MISSING

Luis Garcia

Jitney Books

#MADEINDADE

#MIAMIFULLTIME

For Gaby and Lexy

MISSING

TABLE OF CONTENTS

Master Printer

"Okay, lemme esplain to jou somesing, my son: Jou no fine a yob, I no pay for eschool. Pero jou fine a yob, any yob, and I pay for jour eschool to the finish. Okay?"

That's my dad.

So I'm like, Okay.

Already it looks like I'm planning to stay in college for the rest of my life anyway. It's only my first year, my second semester, actually, but still, I already know. It's the place to be, I'm telling you. *Art and Shamanism. Chemistry in Society. Woody Allen Cinema. Intro to Pharmacology.* These are the entries I have highlighted in this upcoming fall's catalog. *Jewelry Making. Figure Drawing. Women's Studies.* I don't know about you, but I see endless possibilities here.

Figure all I need to make a day is at least ten dollars for my dose. Everything else's negotiable — food, gas, weed — surely these things'll work themselves out. Like Dad's not gonna let me starve is he? And like how am I to drive to school or work without gas? A little pot dealing never hurt anyone.

Right.

*

Driving along in my bubble of pot smoke I see passing in front of a Blockbuster Video store a guy dressed like a VHS tape standing on the sidewalk waving at me.

I pull over and watch him...

I can get a job like that. Yeah, I can get a job like that and then, after my first paycheck, quit, stealing the costume to boot. Then I can find another similar job and do the same thing. Over and over and over again. Until I amass a bunch of different costumes. Like say a chicken, and an ice cream cone, and a French fry. Then I can recruit friends to dress up. Like...The Far Out Pointless Mascot Brigade: The Gorilla, The

Camera, The Hot Dog, The Giant Wad of Cotton Candy. We descend on nightclubs and dance. We crash parties. Carry out panty raids. Hold pointless silent vigils at rallies. We stage public fights. Imagine a slice of pizza and a pencil throwing hands in the street, a black and white stripe-shirted gorilla between them.

On the Blockbuster Video Tape Man's blue face is a lurid leer.

But happy?

I figure no.

What I seek isn't happy anyway.

*

It doesn't take long.

I find a job as a taco. I'm put to work immediately.

Miami's a hot and humid place, even in T-shirt shorts and flip-flops, but put on a ten-pound costume of foam rubber and plastic and you got you a personal sauna.

In minutes I'm drenched, sloshing around in my Chucks. Every hour or so the Viva Taco manager dude sends out a yellow-visored pimply-faced high school kid to make sure I get a water break and not die on them up in here.

But I'm fine, thanks, keeping good THC and H$_2$O levels...

I'm five hours on the sidewalk, waving at cars my green leafy lettuce arms, dancing my green leafy lettuce legs, and rocking a huge smile too. Not because I'm required to, my face hidden behind a screen-like flap of pretend shredded cheddar cheese, but because this is a blast!

It's not happiness, surely, but close.

"Great job today," goes my new boss helping me out the back of the taco. "I like the dancing."

I go, Thanks. Tomorrow, same time?

*

At home I make a sandwich with sandwich gear Dad's got in the fridge: ham, cheese, lettuce, tomato, mayo and mustard on whole wheat bread, whole thing in the toaster oven, kosher dill on the side.

Eating at the kitchen table I fill out an old Master Card application. Where it says Occupation I write Student / Taco.

*

My fourth day, I sneak the costume into my truck, take it home. I'm not planning to steal it just yet, first paycheck's still a few days away, I just can't wait anymore to take pictures of it, put Rachel in it and photograph her by the lake by my house. Or anywhere. Because a giant taco looks great no matter where you put it.

I'm in the living room, inside the taco, checking myself out dancing in the mirror. I got salsa loud on the stereo. Frankie Ruiz.

But then all of a sudden Dad's home. He opens the door, stops, stands in the doorway holding his briefcase, his jacket slung over it. He's got this yellow and green paisley tie on loose around his collar, open, and he's suddenly slack-jawed.

I run over to the stereo, shut it off with the tip of my lettuce arm.

He goes, "Pero te volviste loco o que?"

I flip up my shredded cheddar cheese mask and go, Uh, no. It's for work.

Then he goes, "Pero...What do jou do at work?"

And I'm like, Wave at cars.

He sets down the briefcase, takes a step forward, into the house. Then he throws up his arms and goes, "Dass no a yob comemierda!"

I go, You said any job, Dad.

"Pero jou haf brains! Jou're in kallesh!" he goes. "Dass a yob for people dat haf mental prollems! Jou are not a retarded!"

I go, Dad. Don't overreact. It's just a job.

"Yust a yob!" he goes. "Yust a yob!" Then he's like, "I am no going to pay for jour kallesh if jou are going to work like a taco! Okay!"

And I'm like, But.

*

I'm sitting on the bed in my room. My green lettuce legs jut straight out in front of me. Soon Rachel comes in. Rachel's my girlfriend. She has red hair and blue eyes. She's the prettiest most understanding girl in the world. Considering she's still with me.

She goes, "Cool costume."

But I don't say anything.

Then she goes, "Hey. What's wrong?"

I don't wanna talk about it, I go, and flip down my shredded cheddar cheese.

"Oh, poor baby," she goes and comes and sits down next to me. "Talk to me, sweetie."

I can feel her stroking gently my tortilla shell.

*

Days pass and I'm still jobless. Dad's getting on my case. I bitch about it to Rachel but she just stares at me not saying anything.

We're sitting outside Dairy Queen. I'm demolishing a banana split watching Rachel lick chocolate shell off a derby. Her tongue looks like a strawberry.

All of a sudden her face opens up and she's like, "Hey! I got it!" She goes, "Why don't you try that photo lab, the one by the campus. I think they're hiring, dude."

I look at her.

"It's totally you," she goes.

A bite of banana split stops midflight.

Totally me, I think.

Then I think, She's right.

Plus it'll be a neat arrangement. It's in the shopping plaza right next door to the clinic.

*

The place is called Print Masters, A Professional Photolab. The owner's name is Beverly, a chunky lady with squinty eyes and really red hair. I apply.

She interviews me in her office, which is tiny. Between us on this impossibly cluttered desk is a little placard thing facedown atop a box I can't tell is empty or not of Animal Crackers. I don't know why, but I really wish I knew what it said. The placard.

With nothing to write with or on she asks me questions: Am I in school? How are my grades? My GPA? Do I have an interest in photography? It is an internship I seek? And even what was the last book I read.

I answer honestly, trying but not trying too hard to land this job. I keep wanting to flip up the placard, but I restrain myself.

Her hands are doing something on her lap under the desk. She goes, "So, you...don't have a résumé?"

And I'm like, Well, I considered that, considered just making one up, but that'd be lying, because I've never actually had a real, like...job before. Which is in itself kind of a lie. But I don't tell her that, obviously.

Then she smiles a smile I can't honestly say is pretty and goes, "Full time or part time?"

Full time.

"Full time it is then," she goes and gets up and out of her office. I follow. She goes, "You'll be working with Jeff." I look and see Jeff sitting there looking like, Great. He rocks a long graying ponytail and little round spectacles. He looks tall, even seated. "You can start training today if you want," she goes, "but tomorrow come in wearing something with a collar. And your jeans shouldn't be all ripped like that. They have to at least look sorta new." But I can wear sneakers, she says, because I'll be standing up a lot. Then she tells me to go in the back there and find a lab coat that fits and give it to Gloria, who'll put my name on it.

So I go in the back there and try on lab coats until I find one that fits and give it to Gloria, an elfin feathery blond chick I've seen hanging around the shopping plaza smoking cigarettes.

I like the whole lab coat idea. It's gonna have my name on it.

*

In the morning I'm at the clinic first thing, first in line actually.

"Morning, Manny. You're early today. What's up?"

That's Angela, my methadone-dispensing goddess, as she slides my little bottle of cherry-flavored narcotic through the slot under the steel bars. I got a job at Print Masters, I go. Full time printer.

"Really?"

Yup.

"Well, congratulations."

Thanks, I go and take my medicine and leave.

*

I'm early. I wait outside and burn one in the truck until Jeff pulls up. Then I go meet him at the door.

He goes, "Morning, Manny."

And I'm like, Mornin.

But Jeff's eyebrows come crinkly together. Sniffing the air between us he goes, "Is...Is that...Jesus, Manny, you smell like a humongous joint. Don't let Beverly catch you smelling like that. She'll fire you in a heartbeat."

I go, No shit, hey. Thanks.

I sit on my truck's hood smoking a Camel chain. From here I can see all the junkies slink in and out of the clinic, out and back to their cars and rides. Already I feel all fuzzy and warm inside, the sky changing a million colors in minutes while cars shush by in the street.

Jeff pokes his head out the door. He goes, "Think you're safe now, bub."

I hop down, drop the Camel, squash it into the blacktop under the right one of my freshly laundered Chucks.

*

Second day training I already got this down. The 1-hour machines are mine. It comes natural. Gradations of colorant primaries, subtractive magenta, yellow, cyan.

Jeff steps back and away and in minutes I got it spitting out piles and piles of 4 x 6 and 5 x 7 color and black-and-white prints.

It's a lot to see here. I realize. Rachel was right. Totally me.

And when Beverly and Gloria arrive Jeff goes, "Manny's a natural. Look at him go."

I don't look up. Prodigies don't break their concentration easy.

"Give him his lab coat."

You mean my cape.

I expect Gloria to like slip it on me but no, I have to actually stop to put it on.

I hold it out in front of me, at arm's length like a soiled diaper, and go, Uh, this isn't my name.

It says *Danny, Print Masters Printer*

"Oh. Whoops," goes the dumb blonde.

I'm still holding it out. Kind of pissed.

Beverly goes, "Oh don't worry about that. Give it here. Gloria will fix it tomorrow."

I work the whole day without my coat, feeling jilted. But tomorrow will be better. I'm gonna look sharp in my good-as-new Chucks, my Levi's, my bright red Lacoste shirt and my super white lab coat with my name on it. I feel like asking Beverly could she have it read Master Printer instead of just Printer.

But no.

In time.

*

At my job I kill hours printing people's photos. What a catalog, this life. Sticky cake-faced kids in party hats and wild sugar eyes. Starry-eyed couples in front of Eiffel Towers, Gizan Pyramids, Statues of Liberty. Friends propping Leaning Pisa's, flashing V's and signs of peace. Cows and horses on pastures, Anyplace America. Big fat women all oiled-up on the sand like beached whales. Dogs and cats, playing or fighting, can't tell and it doesn't matter. And all these happy accidents, cameras going off unintentionally: A dog's blurred mug pawing the shutter. A kid's-eye-view of a mom's spectral figure giving chase.

And I have feelings I've never felt.

My heart an egg boiling in water.

Falling almost in love.

A sort of Peeping Tom.

I am.

*

"So how do you like it?" goes Rachel.

We sit sucking thick fresh fruit shakes on a wooden bench watching giant ancient tortoises munch lettuce heads. Rachel's got a thin red with white polka dot scarf on tight around her neck, pointless but for its flair. The scarf.

I go, Dude it's the best job on the planet. I'm the ultimate voyeur there. Looking in.

We can hear distant children, the crunch of vegetables.

She goes, "Lemme taste."

And I'm like, I got an idea.

"Hold mine," she goes and takes my cup.

It's art, though humble, in its purest form, I go, babe.

*

I am the one who gets to look in on those intimate moments of your life, moments you and yours alone share. But you never really think about me. Looking in. Moments you think only you get to see.

*

I start printing doubles of the good shots, stealthily slipping them into the pockets of my lab coat, taking them home.

The best shots are accidents. Like the one of the setting sun on a horizon askew through a car's grimy rear window, a milky orange cast to it. Next frame on the roll's the pretty postcard sunset picture they intended to take, which sucks totally.

It's pictures like these I don't have to worry about printing doubles of, surely to be rejected, relegated to the shred bin.

The shred bin's my treasure chest. I pillage daily.

But soon Beverly starts noticing. She goes, "The rejects have been pretty light these days," to no one in particular. Hoping she attributes it to my excellent printing I pretend not to hear. But just in case, after sorting through the rejects at home, I bring my rejects back, dropping them furtively into the bin, piecemeal so there's a little more each day.

*

Rachel's modeling for me espadrilles, going, "So, be honest."

And I'm like, I like. Cuz I like her toes and her toenails' livid red.

Then in the mirror I see her. She's behind me, behind Rachel, facing away from me but in the mirror facing me. I turn around to look. It's the girl from the picture.

I turn and go, Hey little missy...

In the picture she juggles three oranges, her hair up in honey nut pigtails, her electric-blue T the inverse to orange. The background's all lush earth tones: healthy green lawn, live oak leaves dripping down from the top of the frame, and in the back a chain link strangled in kudzu. The colors pop as if neon-painted, the way I imagine color TV looked during its advent. All three oranges are frozen in midair. You can tell she won't catch them all, biting her little red tongue poking out her lips. The photo's all tension and joy. I have it at home.

...how's that juggling comin along?

She stops, looks at me googly-eyed, her mouth open.

She goes, "Huh?"

Then all of a sudden her mom comes and snatches her hand up and drags her away still looking at me.

I go, Bye.

Watching her get tinier and tinier into the crowd of the mall, waving at me.

Then Rachel goes, "You know her?"

And I'm like, Yeah.

*

I start seeing pictures of small dead animals — lizards, mice, sparrows, etcetera — all usually on a welcome mat or a leaf-littered driveway or a raw concrete sidewalk. There are lots of them. All of them aerial views. Back to back to back on the roll. Something about them. Never any sky or sense of up or down but always different times of day. You can tell by the lengths of shadows. Uniform, coherent matter-of-fact documents of little morbid trophies. Presents. Damn good work.

They're for a Mrs. Jennifer Delgado.

I wait for her.

I go, These pictures are really great Missus Delgado.

Probably in her mid-thirties she's slim and attractive in green scrubs and big trendy sunglasses.

"Thanks but they're not really mine," she goes. "My son takes them. I got him a camera for his eighth birthday and, sheesh, now he's taken to this craze. I don't know what's gotten into him. Personally I think it's gross."

They're actually really good though. If you look. Good composition, lighting, coherence. He's thinking visually. It's tight. I see lots of pictures, Missus Delgado, but not many like this. In fact, I thought this was some college art student's work but, you say he's eight? Jeez. If this ain't the acumen of greatness I don't know what is.

"Really? You think?"

Sure of it. Comes natural to him. It seems. You might have a little genius on your hands, Missus Delgado.

*

Today's a week later. She brings him in.

"Here's my little genius," she goes. "Say hi, Luca."

"Hi."

Just like his mom he has black eyes and black hair and the small mouth and pointy chin of an anime cartoon.

I pull his photos from the envelope. Lemme show you my favorite one, Luca. Look. See this one here, how all the little leaves make like a big explosion, and the tail makes a neat swirl.

"Yeah," he goes.

And look at the guts.

"It's like a little brain."

Exactly.

"Cool."

No. Totally cool. Keep up the good work, I go, and slide him his pictures across the Formica top.

Mrs. Delgado thanks me, pays, and they leave.

Then Beverly comes and tells me what I did was nice, that I should have a kid.

*

Print Masters has an Anything Goes policy. Meaning people bring in porn. Both soft and hard, but mostly soft. The only thing we're supposed to report to the authorities is anything that looks "almost questionable."

Almost Questionable is Beverly's term.

Jeff and I are alone in the lab.

We pull out all the porn, check it out.

"Wow, Manny. Look at this lady. She's huge."

Yeah. I counted four vaginas.

"Stop it."

With a possible fifth.

"That's gross."

No dude. Check this lady. She's like a million.

"Oh my god that's Missus Anderson."

Missus Anderson could pass for a mummy in this one.

"Stop. I don't wanna see anymore."

No, no. Check these out. Now is that incredible or what?

"I — "

All I can think is stick figure. Next to her.

"That's amazing."

Yeah.

But no.

Because what's amazing is Ms. Vasquez has apparently hired a professional to take her naked modeling pictures. The lighting is good, the exposures perfect, every detail showing nicely. In the last month I've seen literally hundreds of images of her. In every possible pose. Always alone on a bed or a chair, or on a sheet on the floor. Sometimes right on the carpet.

The lady is gorgeous. Very short hair like a boy, dark brown, frowsy, like windswept, but with nothing boyish about her. Anfractuous hips and ass on down and waistless. Calves strong and shapely, tits like enormous globes. Sometimes I get a boner, but I can't jack off here. I fuck her with my mind. When I'm inside Rachel.

Once during my lunch break at McDonald's across the street in came Ms. Vasquez. I was sitting eating. I watched her in line, stripped her mentally and then watched her eat a Big Mac in nothing but Nikes.

I've got this one picture of her. She's crawling across a plush red carpet, back arched, ass in the air, arms fully extended with her palms flat on the floor, but still her nipples are nearly dragging on the carpet.

I've got this one on my wall.

*

Two months pass and I amass about three hundred photos. Give or take. All 4 x 6 color prints. I arrange and re-arrange them in a tight grid on a wall in my room. Actually, it takes up one whole wall, floor to ceiling and half of another.

It's huge. Really something.

But I don't know. Maybe I'm deluded. Maybe it's not such a great idea after all. So I look at it high and I look at it sober and I try being hard on myself. But damn, it still looks good.

*

"I like what you're doing, Manny."

Rachel's got this sexy husky voice. That with the way her last syllable of every sentence sort of drops like drives me nuts.

I go, Really? You think it works?

"Yeah," she goes, walking slowly back and forth in front of it, her hands behind her. "Looks pretty solid. Like what's happening. It's chaotic and slipshod at first glance but...imposing. And like arranged by color and content...Dude it really melds now looking at it close. It's a big random slice of life made up of a bunch of little random slices of life."

It's intimate, I go.

"Exactly," she goes. "And real. And also some of the photos are actually really good. Like this one here with the kid in the Superman costume. I mean he's really flying."

He's on a trampoline.

"Awesome."

I know.

"But I don't know though, Manny. What about the whole like plagiarism issue?"

Not an issue. This is readymade.

"Yeah. I guess...I guess you have a point there."

Course I have a point. Plus what the hell does she know? She's all stoned too.

*

"So bro, like check it out, bro, do you like...like acid?"

That's my little sister, Jennifer. We're standing in my mom's kitchen at my mom's house where despite my coming here a lot for free meals and holidays and stuff I've never actually had a room of my own. When I sleep here I sleep on the couch.

And here I am, now, to eat and that's it and here's my sister, in gigantic hoop earrings, a tube top and hot pants, plus I think she's a Latin Queen now or something, coming at me with this shit.

I go, You're selling acid?

And she's like, "Don't tell Mom."

And I'm like, Promise, locking my lips with a pretend key.

But what the hell are you doing selling acid? I go.

Because Jennifer is fourteen.

She goes, "It's not mine it's Papo's. You know Papo, my boyfriend?"

Yeah, Papo. The Latin King guy.

I go, Yeah, I remember.

She goes, "It's white blodder."

And I'm like, Okay. Let's see it.

*

Saturday morning, about six, I drop the four hits I finagled off my sister. Then I go to the clinic and get my dose. Then I come back home, sit in a chair in front of the wall and wait...

Watch...

Listen to the art historian, critic, child, lunatic talk. How pointless it all is. Putting down the work's body's purpose, stealing personal documents, giving meaning meaninglessness...

But it's no use. The more I ponder, watch, the more changes in the coalescing wall's grid and the stranger, stronger my conviction becomes. I am...a sort of demigod of sorts here, tinkering, whose job's existence points only at tipping balance's tender — so tender — murals.

I —

"Oye. Que haces?"

Uh.

"No trabajas hoy?"
Oh shit.

*

Sorry I'm late.
That's me, outside of me, with a smile hurting my face I can't wipe off thinking I think Jeff knows what's up. Jeff, what's up?
"Hey."
I sit at my station to work immediately concealing my looming...insane...
And everyone's lives in my hands now, what I see like a movie, roll after roll, each roll a reel of moving pictures, someone's life. Doing my best making lives colorful again. Because somewhere along these lines the lines have been lost to my job's making, making memories.
Here I am.
Creator of memories in color of color.
The means by which we stop time's coil, the only means to take short breaks and just...look.
Time's breather.
Where time's out of Time.
Proud to be here, part of it, tinkering around, making it all happen...blowing candles off numbers, big bears and dolls of the kewpie or teddy types at carnivals and fairs, private homes, birthdays, balloons at parks...kids swimming and playing and goggles and gap-tooth smiles.
The whole world three colors' gradations, components...tap tap...reds are just right now print...little cyan, that's it...all right plus three magenta, tap, minus one yellow, nice...tap tap...
...kite flyers and ice cream cones, the world's people drinking and licking and smiling and thinking...
"Uh, Manny, these prints are looking kinda magenta."
It's Beverly. Holding a stack of fresh prints.
I go, Really? Lemme see.
"Yeah, look. See for yourself," she goes and hands them over.
And I take them, standing up.

Hm. I guess you're right but it kind of works. Don't you think? Look. They're all pictures of sports cars. I guess it's a car show or something and the images are all crap so why not just like make them all crappy-colored, uniform I thought you know I'm just trying to help with the aesthetics.

"Uh...Just print them again, Manny. And print them right."

Fine. If you say so...

I see Jeff stop and look at me. What am I doing, what am I saying? Crumbling.

...What is right anyway?

And she's like, "What did you say?"

And I'm like, Nothing.

Then she goes, "Okay well, when you're done there come see me. I need your help."

This is ridiculous. I can't help everyone, Beverly. I mean I know our lives are all real messed up and I know it, I know that and I'm really trying my best to help over here but no one sees that, and now neither do you. Is your life all messed up too?

"Uh— "

This place is dark.

"What are you talking about?"

Darkness, lighten up, and I'm talking about what we're talking here, doing here, what's so important you don't see it. No one does. These pictures, they're the world to us too! They should be. We're part! The whole! I go, holding up a stack of garish car photos, shaking them at her. But no, it's just work to you, just money, but this is life is art is life and you don't see it!

"Calm down, Manny."

No. I am calm. Real calm, inside and outside me, I should be running this place. In charge. We're in charge of these people's memories, their lives, these fragile moments and all we have to do is just stop and look. Don't you see, just look! Don't you see that!? L O O...

"Manny? Are you taking drugs?"

Jeff shakes his head at his lap. Beverly is before me, arms akimbo — a-kim-bo — peering at me from slits atop fat cheeks. And there's

Gloria, poking her head out of the back room where she works the slide machine, her mouth hanging open.

I go, You mean besides the methadone?

Beverly's chins jerk back...

Did I just say that?

...and an unsightly crease forms between her...eyes.

She goes, "You're a patient at the methadone clinic?"

Jeff looks up, shakes his head at me.

I go, Um...Nnno.

"Manny. Put those photos down. You're fired."

Wait how can you? I'm your Master Printer! I'm good with kids!

"You're fired, Manny. Gimme the coat."

The coat...but it's my coat! My coat, my name on it! Look!

"Manny. Please."

I'll run outta here with it, grip its lapels, cut under the counter. Go now, but.

No. Hell. Screw it. You can have your damn coat. I already have all I need from you, this place.

I take it off and hand it to her.

You didn't fire me, Beverly. I quit. A long time ago I quit. Like a hundred million years ago I quit and now, I never actually worked here, you'll be nothing.

Nada. Zip. Zero.

Because I...am gone.

These are my words, remember.

And I leave, but I know not where, exactly, because out here, it sure is pretty out here.

Beautiful People

The handsome young man lived with his girlfriend and his roommate and his roommate's girlfriend in an apartment that came to be known in their circle as the Party House. He and his roommate, who was a handsome young man himself, had long talked about buying or leasing or renting a place together. This was before they were roommates, of course, for the handsome young man had been living in a warehouse loft with his former band mates — who were neither particularly handsome nor clean nor well-mannered — since he moved out of his parents' house when he was nineteen. But that had only lasted about a year, maybe a little more, before the band started to break slowly up and he decided that such an arrangement was not actually particularly fun at all to live in, what with all their living like bums squatting with no hot water or anything remotely like a kitchen or a washer or a dryer or even a real front door, or even a normal shower that was not a Port-o-Potty like shower they bought at Home Depot that ran only really cold water, and the ever present fuggy rank unnamable smell of rotting socks or something they lived with, and the mess that was a mess like no other ever found indoors, an industrially dirty, beer-mud-on-the-concrete-floor-type mess of the kind you would expect to find in the lot on the day after a carnival or a fair, and this was like every day, the mess, but for the handsome young man the worst part of it all was the embarrassment of having to go back to his parents' house to sleep and shower once a week, or so, for some semblance of normalcy or, better said, respite from what seemed like a great big giant step backwards in life. And so the handsome young man began to conspire with a college friend of his (the would-be roommate) who was lucky enough to still be living with his parents, and together they searched for the right place for six months (that felt like forever). It was the handsome young man's soon-to-be roommate who did most of the searching, online and in the papers, since it was the handsome young man who lived in the front-doorless, Internet-accessless, caveman-like bum squalor with his stupid loud-farting sock-smelling beer-drinking pot-smoking keg-standing bong-clearing friends in that stupid air-conditionedless bad idea with an indoor trampoline and a rope swing attached to the twenty-foot ceiling, and the soon-to-be roommate had made a list of places they drove around to. There were places too close to the hood, and some even *in* the hood, and there were places right next door to methadone clinics and hourly-rate motels and homeless shelters and halfway houses and rehabs and, really, it was not looking good at all until the very last place they walked into. It had two bedrooms and dark wooden floors and a kitchen with a bar in both the living *and* dining rooms, and not just one or two or even three but *four* doors this apartment had, doors from the kitchen and living room out to the front balcony-slash-porch, and doors from what would be their bedrooms out to the back balcony-slash-porch, and it had a big bathroom too that they would share, and the neighbors they saw around seemed nice and good-looking waving at them from afar as if they knew them, and plus and also the landlord, who was showing them around, and who was a not at all bad-looking young man himself, would be their downstairs neighbor. So they put down and moved in, bought some cool secondhand furniture at Goodwill and at the Salvation Army, picked up a few nice giveaways they found on Craigslist, brought their old stereos and stuff from their old rooms at home, and their parents bought them and even gave them some basic necessities from their own homes too like towels and linens and pots and pans and plates and cups and spoons and forks and knives and even a toaster and a blender and a microwave oven, and with all this stuff they were happy, occasionally celebrating with beers and high fives in their new kitchen.

At the time they moved in, the handsome young man and the handsome young man's roommate were both single or just sort of dating, but they did not remain single or just sort of dating for long. Within months they each had steady girlfriends, and the girlfriends happened to be best friends, to each other, that is, and they were both very beautiful young ladies. It was not long before the girls moved in with them and the fervor for interior decorating really began to unfold and quickly became a communal effort that brought them all closer together as friends or even like a little family, one might say, and soon the apartment took on a very stylish yet DIY look as diverse as their individual personalities, expressed through strategically placed computers and LCD screens all over the place, photographs taped with masking tape directly to the walls, orchids, and the one or two potted mind-altering plants, plus other plants, and the throw rugs and the bookshelves stacked with high-minded literature and *National Geographic* magazines, and the arcane scientific and technologic textbooks only someone like the handsome young man's roommate might actually be caught reading, and the weird knick knacks and conversation pieces of the old-school-type like Rubik's Cubes and Chia Pets and Pet Rocks, and the Battleship and Candyland games for the entertainment of idle times, and also the handsome young man's old record player and impressive indie and punk rock record collection laid out neat and orderly (and not just for show), and when the handsome young man's roommate's girlfriend's parents gave them an old antique-like matching dining room and coffee table set that matched all so perfectly with the apartment's dark wooden floors and bars they were really, really happy because it seemed to like tie all their efforts together, somehow, and that very night they celebrated with beer and wine and pot and laughs and hors d'oeuvres the girls had made and then, later on, sex.

It was the place to be. Over time they hosted dinner parties, Halloween parties, birthday parties, event after parties, Secret Santa parties, unfriendly domino tournaments that got physical and friendly poker tournaments that went nowhere, plus potlucks and front balcony-slash-porch barbecues and slumber parties and independent movie screenings, and it was also the pre-beach going gathering spot and the post all-night clubbing crash site too, a refuge for too-drunk-to-drive-homers and on New Year's, well, you could just imagine. By this time there were four keys out — one for the handsome young man and one for the handsome young man's girlfriend and one for the handsome young man's roommate and one for the handsome young man's roommate's girlfriend. But then one day one of the handsome young man's girlfriend's girlfriends decided to move out of the city to another city on the whole other side of the country to live with one of her many cross-country boyfriends, only to within less than a week break up with this boyfriend and then have to come back all brokenhearted with nowhere to stay, and so she was given a key and invited to sleep on the couch. It was around this same time that one of the handsome young man and the handsome young man's roommate's friends, who worked as a first mate on a tall ship sailing the high seas, came around asking could he like maybe sleep on their floor or their couch when he was in their city on shore leave. These were all beautiful people, the handsome young man and his girlfriend and his roommate and his roommate's girlfriend, so naturally they gave him a key too, without question. But then it was not long before the handsome young man's girlfriend's girlfriend found herself a new boyfriend who actually lived in their own city this time, and whose parents had a very recent and devastating financial thing involving the foreclosure of a home and the repossession of lots of stuff, effectively putting him out on his ass, he said, and so he too got a key. Then a few months later there came their all mutual and pretty much famous friend who had spent the last five years of her life after high school touring the United States of America by broken down car after broken down car funded solely by her efforts as a solo musician, and so obviously she got a key too. So now there were eight keys out — one for the handsome young man and one for his girlfriend and one for his roommate and one for his roommate's girlfriend and one for his girlfriend's girlfriend and one for his girlfriend's girlfriend's boyfriend and one for the sailor and one for their hardworking musician friend who was pretty much famous — and for a long time it remained at eight keys out, even after the sailor had one day come home with a sailor girlfriend of his, because this particular sailor girlfriend of his was definitely not and by no means getting a key too. She didn't need one. And it was around this time that the Party House moniker was dubbed, though not by anyone who actually lived there, meaning anyone in possession of a key. No one who ever actually lived there called it the Party House. It was a term flung absently about in their circle but not in the house, which was technically not even a house but an apartment.

The handsome young man would sometimes come home from work — for by this time they were all, by the way, the handsome young man and his girlfriend and his roommate and his roommate's girlfriend, all out of school and working successfully, or something like that, in their respective artsy DIY-promoting and freelance computer programming and fashion-designing and event-coordinating fields — he would come home from work to a full house having a party on full blast. This coming-home-to-a-bunch-of-what-were-essentially-fucking-strangers-mostly experience was not limited only to the handsome young man, but his girlfriend and his roommate and his roommate's girlfriend had all also experienced it once or twice or hell fucking lots of times. But they were not complaining about it, really, not necessarily, they would say, it was just, you know, kind of unexpected sometimes.

So anyway the handsome young man's mind had one day started to wander slowly off from his home life or apartment life or whatever, and from his girlfriend, too, and even from his friends in general, so that he began to busy himself forging relationships with his neighbors, of which there were six in the building — the landlord who lived right below, the gay couple who lived right behind the landlord, the lesbian couple who lived right above the gay couple, and the very attractive girl everyone suspected was either a call girl of some sort of a stripper who lived almost like central to all of them in the building — and his busy forging of these relationships he could not have explained aside from the sheer boredom of the almost sometimes overwhelming social circle or network he seemed to suddenly find himself at the center of or maybe like realize was there all around him, for there were in fact times when relationships were strained in the house or apartment or whatever the fuck you want to call it between him and his roommate and between him and his roommate's girlfriend and between his girlfriend and his girlfriend's girlfriend and between his roommate's girlfriend and his girlfriend's girlfriend's boyfriend and between the sailor and the pretty much famous hardworking musician and even between him and his own girlfriend whom he believed he truly loved. And so, even though these strains tended to slacken or blow over they still took an emotional sort of subconscious or what have you, like, toll.

These things went on for almost two years, the strained and almost even bad times escalated, buffered by the good times and the parties and the sex and the games and the just plain good old good-natured get-togethers on holidays and paydays. And during this time the handsome young man had busily expanded his own personal circle of friends to include his neighbors, who began to regularly show up when the Party House's noise level rose, like for instance at the Halloween party when the gay couple showed up as twin homosexual Tarzans all greased-up and the lesbian couple as pink-clad drag queen ninjas, or like on Christmas at the Secret Santa party they showed up with gifts to trade or at potlucks with food to share. Nobody wondered what was up or who would invite them even, but whatever, because the things going on happened behind doors not theirs that were closed.

Except of course for the handsome young man's girlfriend, who did wonder. She was by far the most levelheaded of the bunch and, maybe even, the most beautiful. So anyway she one day took it upon herself to borrow her mother's friend's daughter's car so she could be, you know, like QT on the DL when she came and parallel parked it up the street from their building in a spot that afforded a clear sightline, more or less directly, to almost all of the building's doors. Surely too far to be seen, but just as she had suspected, too far also to see clearly all the building's doors herself, she had the foresight to borrow or more like steal the handsome young man's really expensive bird watching binoculars so as to see what exactly went down. This was on a day the handsome young man had off from work, and she had left early that morning (he was still asleep in bed naked) under the pretense that she was going to work. She had already planned this day off for a whole week for this very reason: to leave in her own car to her mother's house to borrow her mother's car real quick, to then go to her mother's friend's house and borrow her mother's friend's daughter's car, for the honest reason she gave but that no one had honestly believed and here she was, spying — just as she had told her mother and her mother's friend and her mother's friend's daughter, to spy on her boyfriend — spying, with binoculars and everything. Though she felt badly about spying, she really felt she had no choice, for there were in her mind reparations to be made. The handsome young man's girlfriend's intentions were indeed less confrontational than conciliatory in nature. Nip this in the bud, she reasoned, watching that morning through his binoculars the handsome young man exit their apartment's front door and go downstairs and knock on the landlord's door. It opened and in he went and stayed in for almost but not quite a whole hour before he came out through the doorway where the landlord now stood smiling leaning against the doorjamb in only a leopard print towel around his waist. Then she watched the handsome young man go directly around to the gay couple's apartment and knock, and she knew they were home because they worked from home and their car was there, and in there the handsome young man went and stayed for almost two hours. It had not occurred to the handsome young man's girlfriend to pack a lunch, who would have thought? And she grew hungry, but she could not move, for her curiosity and wonder and awe were piqued, to say the least.

When the handsome young man came out of their apartment he was adjusting his clothes in a way only she knew meant he had just put his clothes back on. She then watched him go upstairs to, could it be? Yes, the lesbian couple's apartment. The handsome young man's girlfriend knew here in this case too that only one of the couple was home, namely the cuter one with the dreads who worked as a DJ-slash-bartender, and into their door he went and stayed exactly one hour. That the handsome young man's girlfriend had a natural bent or sensitivity for the concinnity in all things, and was supernaturally understanding, and that she was not a jealous person — one of those rare truly not jealous persons who really truly knows no jealousy on account of an unwavering faith in their love, and knew that the handsome young man's actions had nothing to do with love but rather had all to do with the boredom she felt she knew he felt, and something else like a subconscious yearning for change in his life — and that she truly, truly loved him and wanted to marry him and was about three or four months pregnant with their child, helped the whole situation: she sitting there hungrier than a mother and just literally unbelieving of the fact that her boyfriend, the handsome young man, father of her child, was actually fucking literally everyone in the building, watching it all unfold through the binoculars he used to watch fucking birds. Watching him come out of the lesbians' apartment doing his little idiosyncratic post-coitus clothing adjustments was all she needed to see, really, but she kept watching anyway to see if — as she had initially suspected, the whole reason she was here in the first place — to see if he would go into, yes, he was going into the very attractive suspected call girl-slash-stripper's apartment. Through the binoculars the handsome young man's girlfriend-slash-new baby momma saw the very attractive suspected call girl-slash-stripper answer the door in just a T-shirt and mouth the words, how much time we got, before he went in and disappeared. The handsome young man's girlfriend-slash-new baby momma did not wait to watch him come out but drove off with a Wendy's spicy chicken sandwich in the front of her mind, while thinking in the back of her mind all these other things that would soon change all of their lives. Like how the handsome young man's roommate's girlfriend — who was herself beginning to maybe exhibit symptoms of severe clinical manic depression, or something totally unstable like that, crying and screaming at the air about shit only she could have solved and then barricading herself for days on end in their apartment's bedroom's walk-in closet — had aired to her, the handsome young man's girlfriend-slash-new baby momma, that her boyfriend, the handsome young man's roommate, was maybe, she suspected, using pharmaceutical-grade amphetamines like Ritalin or Dexedrine or something, what with all his whole five-day stints up writing computer programs without blinking, salivating tears down his cheeks, in their room's little spider- and beetle- and just really all types of bug-infested Wild Kingdom that with all its overgrown plants and pot plants and LCD computer screens everywhere looked like a post-apocalyptic NASA control center being reclaimed by Mother Nature, while she hid in the closet crying and screaming manic depressively, subsisting solely on wine, alone in the dark. And how now more people seemed to be living there in the Party House with surely more unsanctioned keys out, including the drunk sailor chick, who was technically not a sailor anymore but who now tended bar full-time while her sailor ex-boyfriend picked up an H habit in Thailand and was now back all nodding inhabiting the couch always. And how things kept turning up missing. And how now there were two or maybe even three ferrets running around foraging the apartment's wildlife that came with all the plants that were now pretty much trees everywhere, and whose ferrets? Well who knew? And plus now if you wanted to come in via the back balcony-slash-porch you needed a machete to like chop your way through the forest there. And how the handsome young man's girlfriend-slash-new baby momma's girlfriend and her boyfriend had taken to recently fighting a lot, throwing at each other breakable shit that was never even theirs to break in the first place. And these were only the top five things on the handsome young man's girlfriend-slash-new baby momma's list of concerns.

So finally that very same day, or very same night, actually, the handsome young man's girlfriend-slash-new baby momma sat the handsome young man down on their bed in their room while she stood and very peacefully and beautifully and diplomatically and non-confrontationally confronted him, sort of jokingly in tone but not really joking at all: Was he really actually sleeping with all their neighbors? And don't lie, babe, she said. But lie he did not, or even think to, for the handsome young man outright confessed, though wordlessly, to what she already knew, and her reaction was to him totally unexpected in that she seemed actually kind of proud of this feat, his ability to be able to easily bone anyone and everyone who laid eyes on him, or vice versa, telling him now in a hushed conspiratorial tone, a tone he knew well, that they maybe should just get the hell out of here, the Party House, meaning, and get their own place far, far away from these people and this town and this scene because babe I'm tired, and I love you, and I know you're tired too of this shit babe. I can see it in your eyes babe but babe listen no listen good there's a good thing here look, touch it, feel here and come you touch it too babe no I know you can't feel I can't feel it either from outside but it's true babe it's true we're not anymore alone.

Burping Birds

I am reluctant to explain to you why I am back here. The reason is so absurd it is difficult for even me to believe. That I am a changed man requires I not tell you so, and to explain would, because of our past, sound beyond absurd, which would, by a turn, equal lie.

An amusing and perhaps beautifully written sentence fragment lies hidden in the tedium of Chapter 33: *Presents nudity in such a way as to create the appearance that sexual contact is imminent, i.e., display of contact or intended contact with genitals, pubic area, or female breasts orally, digitally or by foreign object*...and I am at the moment trying to figure a way to work it in to a story.

What if I told you that, beginning four months ago, every time I sensed a belch, I felt a dry sort of fluttering in my chest, and out of my mouth came a sparrow (*Passer domesticus,* specifically), would you believe me?

Being averse to the Christian propaganda that floats around back here along with the well-thumbed King James Bibles, plus the one or two read and reread trashy, dog-eared, torn sections of cheap drugstore novels considered contraband, I have killed large chunks of Time reading the available portions of Chapter 33, for pleasure, and have begun to wonder, and am surprised and even embarrassed by my naïveté of what exactly Chapter 33 is. Is it out of a book? Is it itself a tome? Is it part of a work of several volumes? If Chapter 33 deals with prison rules and regulations, what does Chapter 1 deal with? Chapter 2? I have decided to figure this out as soon as I am out of confinement.

I remember how, when we first moved into our little house, we discovered that the living room walls' thick paint was not only thick paint but painted-over wallpaper, and when we took that wallpaper down we found more painted-over wallpaper before we got to the actual wall you set to wallpapering with your photographs, way underestimating how much masking tape you would need. The walls in here are similar, only there is no wallpaper but layers and layers of paint of slightly different colors.

The little birds come out alive and well and apparently unharmed and hop happily onto my finger, ruffle their feathers, look at me quizzically, but then soon fly off, for they are by no means tame.

I was going to write to tell you how so far I have had only one celly, who was occupying the cell when I arrived; how he was a Latin gang member classified as a "keep away," meaning keep away from the general population for rioting and hurting others; how his teeth were clean but misshapen and chipped and misaligned and could have benefited from childhood braces; how he bore scars on many parts of his body; how he told me several stories of fighting, and pantomimed as such; how he did not touch me, but how when he used my general position to demonstrate the objects of his stories' foci, I could feel issuing from him a sort of dyslexic frustration; how I told him stories in return; how his eyebrows went synclinal whenever I used polysyllables; how his plans for when he gets out included caring for his three-year-old daughter by smuggling drugs into prison through associations he has made during his stay here, for a big turn-over profit, he implied, which he referred to as "The Lick"...

I was not going to mention it, but at this point I need to, because I am stuck — cobbling together a story about a reality show about the making of a documentary about a family addicted to watching the reality show about the making of the documentary of themselves. I know you have offered to be only my typist, but still: Any ideas?

...how I no longer have a celly and am happy with my newfound peace and quiet; how the chaplain visits my cell door weekly and offers me a Bible; how I tell him I am not Christian and how he asks then what are you...and how I tell him if anything I'm Buddhist; how he gives me the Bible anyway and says here is a King James. Read it; how I have taken to reading it aloud for hours at a time to myself in a mock British accent all *Monty Python*-style; how I find this activity endlessly amusing.

Inmates are not allowed to keep pets of any sort — mice, spiders, snakes, etc. — as explicitly stated in Chapter 33, and consequences include up to thirty days in confinement. Mice and spiders vie for the most commonly kept pets. Guys here have mice born in footlockers. These mice know nothing but peanut butter, saltines, cornbread purloined from the chow hall, chocolate chip cookies, duplexes, Marias and running around the dorm under bunks inside makeshift hamster balls fashioned from discarded Gatorade bottles punched with holes for air. Guys pit their spiders to fight; betting on the outcomes is big — lots of Ramen, mackerel, zoom-zooms and wham-whams to be won. Snakes are rare but not unheard of, birds even more so. Chapter 33 says nothing specifically about birds.

...how to kill Time I share stories in Spanglish through a vent with a guy I don't know in a cell downstairs; how I count bricks and screen holes for fun; how I know exactly how many bricks and screen holes there are in here; how I learned how to make origami with decorative paper the Audubon Society sent me with instructions...

I want to write a story about a footlocker mouse, like, "I was born in a footlocker...," but that is all I have, so far.

...how my passerine eructations suddenly stopped as soon as I got here; how I cannot for the world burp no matter how hard I try...

Last time I was back here it was winter. I'm not sure you remember; you tend to remember things differently than I do. But last time it was winter, and back here there are no heaters, and when the exhaust fans were on I wore my single sheet and blanket like a cloak. There were several obstacles obscuring my view outside. First there were the bars of my cell door, and then in the hall's opposite wall's window where my view mocked there were two layers of tightly woven mesh, and just beyond that horizontal slats made it so that the distant trees and even more distant clouds were not but vague ideas. Sometimes I dreamed of blizzards I have never experienced and woke shivering to my celly's snore.

...how this time it is summer; how it is HOT; how even Beyond Hot is an understatement; how this time I have no such view; how this time it is only a wall; how this wall is painted a mind-numbing institutional colorless color that tries to call itself beige but is not beige; how I stare at this wall for long stretches of Time; how this color has none of the intended soothing effects; how...but decided to not go any further than that.

Burping *birds*? You think it is difficult for you to believe?

I am not sure we are even together anymore; the both of us are guilty of being noncommittal. But still you swim from dream to dream in me. In this way you have gained access to my most sordid corners. And there, I am not sure which words, which images are yours and which are mine. I am over trying to figure it out. Because here we are, being someone new, being someone torn, being someone incredible.

Los Santos

They were sounds she knew: a faucet running, the rainfall of a
shower going, a closing closet door; and she knew exactly which closet
door, which faucet, which shower. In the sepia shades of dreams
Enriqueta saw her younger self's silhouette in the backlit yellow shower
curtain — her hands up in her hair, her brown curls wet, tamed, her thin
arms up at angles. How she looked when she was young. She was not
asleep, but not awake either. In the dream it might have been night.

When she woke it was to the crow of one of her roosters. Her
eyes opened. It was morning. She lay in bed awhile, watching the light
move across the popcorn ceiling. How the glitter winked and the
rhomboid of window light lengthened and stretched and leaned to one
side. She pondered a little the images still pressed in her mind — Mariela
in the shower, the dressmaker's bust naked in her room — but in
seconds the images were gone. She might not have dreamt at all.

She rose from the bed and went to the bathroom. It was a
utilitarian and orderly place. She kept nothing personal out. But inside
the medicine cabinet and the drawer there were many Rx bottles from
CVS and OTC drugs and aides and cosmetics. Since Rafael had died no
one save she and Mariela had been in here, and Mariela only a handful
of times to filch a couple of Xanax.

The bathroom was brighter and quieter than the bedroom. There
was no reason for her to close the door but she did. Enriqueta used the
toilet and took her pills and adjusted her face and brushed her teeth
outside of her mouth. In the mirror she smiled a smile more knowing
than bright.

"Ya estas vieja, vieja," she said.

*

The kitchen windows cast long shadows. She moved about in
the paneled light. There was a quiet stillness in the house, but she knew
she was not the only one awake. She wore a thin cotton nightgown, its

flower pattern fading. As she walked she scared up a little tornado of dust motes, flaring a swirl through two low shanks of planar sun, first one and then the other. She was making coffee. Her terry slippers were pink and worn and susurrus on the parquetry floor.

She stood watching for the first drop to perk from the maker's spout — the Italian kind, old and stained a whole decade of Bustelo — and up it came with a hiss and a black bubble. It always reminded her of the oil she'd never once seen with her own eyes come up from the ground. She poured it into a stainless steel carafe and stood whipping it into sugar with a spoon, making espumita. The special granular sound of this type of metal on metal echoed through the house.

She poured the coffee into a demitasse. She would have no Cuban crackers crushed in it today. Her old but not yet so wrinkled lips kissed the cup's silver rim marred from all the times Mariela had put it in the microwave. Standing in the kitchen Enriqueta drank from her coffee cup coffee very slowly, barely a taste at a time, as the sun's light, already beginning to heat, folded around her.

*

In the backyard three ugly roosters pecked at bugs in the grass. Bugs hopped everywhere — grasshoppers and stinkbugs, katydids and aphids — fleeing. There was a tall wooden fence and a sky-blue pool whose pump had just begun to burble — the Kreepy Krawler starting up. Jets too high to hear slit spears into the sky's no clouds and the sun shone hard, giving everything a sharp edge.

She came out holding a set of large cast iron scissors with black handles. A pair of white Keds stood propped on their toes with their heels against the house wall, laces out. Enriqueta walked past the terracotta around the pool and noticed white and black spots of fresh chicken shit she would later hose off.

Up against the fence in one corner of the yard was a chicken coop made of wood and chicken wire. The hens inside clucked as she came up and opened the coop's top and stood looking at them. There were five white hens. Their heads jerked from side to side, eyes alert and blinking. They each looked at her and then looked away and then back at her still clucking. She cocked her head, stood a long time choosing.

*

The hen didn't protest. Enriqueta was gentle.

The bird was calm. She stood on the concrete slab between the pool deck and the back porch holding the chicken upright by its feet, their scaled warm digits' sharp claws gripping her left pinkie. She held it out in front of her at arm's length and spoke Spanish words under her breath only she and los santos could hear.

With the scissors quick and nearly silent save their metallic *shink,* she lopped the chicken's head off from behind and dropped the bird. It landed on its feet, stepping once on its own head, which then flopped from one side to the other, each eye getting a last look up at the sky's white widening wounds. The bird's body made to flap its wings but seemed to decide against that and went running zigzag spurting blood. She took a few steps in its path, then stopped. The roosters had quit foraging to look on. Bugs knowing too machined for cover like crazy, hiding in blades, under what dirt they could find. The headless chicken made two big circles on the slab, passing close to the house, and on its second pass spattered blood across the flaccid shoes. She took little notice. She was reading the blood in the floor.

*

Mariela was fresh out of the shower. Her hair was still wet. She stepped barefoot through the sliding glass door onto the porch's tile and saw her mother's slippered feet. The blood. She looked at her own feet. She'd watch her step.

Her mom stood with the scissors looking down like some hierophant en bata de casa. The chicken was on its side in the grass flapping uselessly, weakly, not another bird in sight. None of this was new to Mariela. Her mother seemed not to notice her. Juan suddenly entered her mind again briefly but then left. It was as though there was something else besides her plans that she had to tell him but had immediately forgotten what it was because when she walked out toward the slab she saw the red Pollock-like splatter on her shoes.

"Mom! What the hell are you doing!" she said. "Lookit my shoes! Jesus!"

"Calmate, mija," her mother said. She didn't look up from the blood on the floor. "Baja la vos, por favor."

"Goddammit, Mom!" she said. "You're crazy!" She kept looking at the blood on her shoes.

"Por tu vida, vieja," she said, looking at her now. "No seas tonta. Ahora sio."

"But my shoes! You got blood on them!" which finally pushed her mother off her quicio completely.

"¡Ay por dios callate!" the mother said.

"I can't believe this!" the daughter said.

"¡Ya, boba!" her mother screamed. "¡Sal de aquí!"

Mariela stomped her foot slapping wetly on the porch's tile and growled a long M in her mouth as she pulled a martial about face, her dress whirling blue around her knees, and marched back into the house.

*

A bare dressmaker's bust stood in the window in Mariela's room. She had recently dropped out and hated living with her mom still at twenty-six. Plus almost a year and Juan still hadn't mentioned anything. Her break wasn't on any horizon and if something didn't give soon she'd have to make something happen.

She stepped into a pair of plain white rubber sandals. Some of Juan's stuff was still around from yesterday — a button-up shirt, sunglasses, two rolls of film, a pack of Zig-Zags. No pot, though. She looked around for nothing else she could think of and then she grabbed her glasses and purse and keys off the dresser and left.

On her way out she had to pass the room reserved for los santos. It was a room no living human was allowed into. A rule her mom had enforced since forever. In the room were couches with prophylactic plastic covers and antimacassars and creepy dolls. There were candies in salvers and rum in shot glasses and cigars burning in ashtrays. There were statues of the figures that had haunted Mariela's childhood dreams. This room had always been the creepiest thing to her.

She would leave this house.

She shot a glance in, passing the room.

And she cursed all los santos aloud.

*

Meeting Juan at Sergio's for breakfast on Sundays was a new thing. Mariela drove there. It was hot out. Her car's AC didn't work, nor did the radio, and she hated how the dash had a huge swollen crack in it. She hated the whole shitty car, in fact, but the drive soothed her. She drove with the windows down. The wind did things to her hair but she didn't care, it felt nice cooling her face. She tapped her fingers to nothing on the steering wheel.

*

She took a seat at a table outside. Her waitress had a gaunt severe face that recalled an image that had once struck Mariela in an old photo gone yellow. One of Abuelo's maybe. Mariela ordered a café con leche with Cuban toast, watching people come and go. She was the only one sitting outside. Juan was on his way, in a bubble, she knew for sure.

*

The waitress came and set her order down and left. Mariela watched the woman's long black hair. It looked almost blue in the sun. She was skinny, looked sick somehow but pretty, and threw her hips around when she walked. Mariela had seen her here before.

Mariela liked her café con leche dark and without sugar. Juan liked it that way too. He always said it waked him up better. The toast broke in big soggy buttery tears. She dipped it into the coffee. She liked watching how the butter formed beads that swirled a tiny range of ocher and caramel colors in the coffee's surface. It felt like reading.

*

Juan pulled the red Bronco into the lot and parked next to Mariela's blue Camry. Juan was seriously in love with Mariela and seeing her for the first time in a day was probably the greatest pleasure he wasn't totally aware of.

He stepped onto Sergio's outside wooden deck and saw her. He took in her feet in the sandals under the table. She had honest calves. She wore oversized dark sunglasses with white frames and her hair was a mane of brown curls. This was his muse. He took and arranged and re-arranged lots of pictures of her, making a wall of her in his studio. Her electric blue dress had spaghetti string shoulder straps. She had honest shoulders too. Her skin was the color of the coffee she drank.

She smiled. With perfect teeth.

He came and kissed the top of her head. It smelled like fruit — papaya, mango. He touched her shoulder and they kissed lightly on the lips: strawberries and coffee, pot and Mentos on his. He came around and sat across from her.

"Jesus. You stink," she said.

"Really?" he said. "It's loud?"

"You smell like a pound."

"That's understandable."

"Don't jones me," she said.

The waitress came to take their order. She smiled at him but not at her. One of her front teeth was crooked. He ordered in English: the special with eggs over easy and bacon and café con leche with Cuban toast. She ordered in Spanish. The waitress turned and left still writing on the pad.

"What is it with you and that?" he said.

"Comida de puta, my mom calls it. Speaking of my mom..."

She told him about the chicken and the blood and her shoes.

And los santos.

"Shit's getting crazier and crazier, Juan. It was never this bad."

"How do you mean?"

"Since Dad died. She's not over it. She hasn't dealt or accepted. Says she has but she hasn't. She keeps doing more and more for him."

"Do you believe it?"

"Please."

"You don't think it's real? Like in any way?"

"It's not real. It's crazy."

He paused. "Yeah."

"I need outta there, Juan."

"Does she ever talk about it? I mean like — him?"

"No."

"What're you gonna do?"

"What do you mean what am I gonna do? Nothing. I have to live there. Maybe I'll kill myself."

"Come on, Mari."

"Or drink myself to death."

"Chill out, babe, please."

She didn't speak her every thought. The sun blared around their table's parasol. It was a dog ear ring heat, an audible scorcher. People came and went. No one sat outside with them.

The waitress came and set their plates down. Again she smiled at him but not at her. She seemed to make a point of this. Mariela took the squeezable Heinz ketchup bottle and gave her sunny-side-up eggs a long downward squirt and then too many shakes of Tabasco. Then she took her fork and started to chop and fold the eggs and ketchup and Tabasco into the rice for a color he couldn't name. All this he watched, not touching his food, and by now the waitress had gone and Juan's smile had grown huge.

They ate in silence.

*

"Algo mas?" said the waitress.

"No," Juan said, "gracias. La cuenta, por favor."

She produced a stack of receipts from one of the front pockets of her apron and found theirs and handed it to Juan and smiled. Then she cleared the table of everything save what was there before so that it looked as though they'd never been there.

"I gotta run," Juan said. "Gotta go do something."

"Okay...Do you have any bud you can spare?" she said.

"Yeah. In the truck." Juan peeled a five from a wad and left it under the saltshaker. "Can you meet me at my place later?"

"Sure, what time?"

"Like — like four or five hours from now," he said.

She looked at her watch, a little insignificant white thing on her wrist. "Okay," she said.

*

Standing between his truck and her car they made out deeply. The parking lot's blacktop was hot and made the air just above it shimmer. Mariela had to stand on her tiptoes to kiss Juan and the soles of her sandals came up between the asphalt and the soles of her feet. One of his hands was completely lost in her hair.

Juan opened the Bronco's passenger door and leaned in and stayed leaning in for what felt like a long time to her, standing there, hand on hip, right foot out, and when he came out he came out with an Altoid tin. Mariela extended her hand palm up and there he placed it. He gave her his entire head. It was all he had for personal use.

*

On his way to a friend's house in Little Havana to make a delivery Juan stopped at a four-way stop and noticed the severed head of a goat at the base of a live oak on the corner. He put the truck in neutral and stepped on the E brake and got out. There were no other cars around. He took a few steps toward it and squatted in front of the curb.

The goat's head's eyes were open. They were black and dull and looked like old cloudy marbles. The head sat in the dirt on a crumpled plastic bag. Flies buzzed and jumped from lips to nostrils and back. The goat's tongue hung pink and wet out to one side. Not a fly was on it and it seemed to sweat. Its front teeth showed perfect square white chompers. Juan had never actually seen anything like this before. He crouched a long time looking.

*

Armando went to the domino park every Sunday. He walked in shade pools cast by the suspended storms of trees and hidden birds singing in them. He wore a white gabardine suit and fedora and walked with a cane. The heat bounced off him.

He stopped cattycorner to where Juan crouched studying the goat head. Armando leaned both hands on his cane to watch.

Juan went to the truck and came back to the curb with his camera. He took several pictures from different angles — crouching, walking around it a few paces, crouching again. He stood close to it to take a couple of aerial shots. Then he hung the camera over his shoulder by the strap and took out his cellphone and photographed it with that.

Armando watched. Shapes of memories of his children rose from the fog in his mind. There was a daughter. Two sons. His eldest had been a photojournalist and had died on assignment in Afghanistan but this fact had been relegated to a sort of trash bin in his mind and in the back of it he began to wonder about when he had last seen him or the other two but in every case it had been too long a time. It was all gone in the second he felt to tell the young man he shouldn't photograph such things. But in the end he said nothing.

Armando stood several minutes after Juan had got in his truck and left. Then he turned and walked back the way he came, unaware of having forgotten what he was on his way to go do. Halfway up the block he stopped to light a cigarette and then kept walking.

*

Outside his little apartment Armando stood and finished the cigarette. His apartment was on the first floor of a yellow two-story building of several apartments and out front were many live oaks and ficus trees and from one of the ficus trees a boat-tailed grackle swooped down and landed on the sidewalk behind him. The bird's black feathers were iridescent with metallic blues and greens in spots of sun that had escaped the tree's trappings as the bird strutted looking for something to eat. Armando dropped the cigarette on the sidewalk and crushed it under his boot and walked off and then here came the bird to inspect it.

Inside Armando hung his hat and cane and went to his desk and opened a drawer. It was a shiny wooden desk, dustless and old and the drawers' tracks ran wood on wood and inside one he found a stack of old photos. They were yellowing with rounded corners. Most if not all of the people in the pictures were dead. He began to thumb through them, shuffling the front one neatly over to the back, unsure of what exactly he looked for. In the back of his mind he hoped it would come to him.

The Screamer

—No...No, but you don't think it's mean?

—Mean...?

—Yeah, mean.

—Mean? Whadaya mean *mean*?

—*Mean.* I mean, like what he's doing to her just to get rid of her.

—Well, I don't know but from what I gather she's being a little more than stubborn or hard to get rid of, and as it turns out she's really dense and, and you know no, no, no now that I think about it no, it's not that mean. It could be worse. Actually, I've seen worse.

—Worse!? No! How? Come on! Poor girl I mean. I mean no listen. Listen all he has to do is talk to her. Tell her it's not working out and stuff like that. These things take patience, diplomacy in a way and worse? Whadaya mean *worse*?

—I mean *worse*.

—Worse than Diego?

—Oh yeah, yeah way worse than Diego. Makes Diego look sweet in fact.

—I don't believe it.

—Believe it, babe...Babe hey you gonna eat that? he said, indicating with a fork the remnants on her plate and at her head's shake no he reached, stabbed, dragged a tangle of angel hair to turn once, twice, three times mopping the oily green sauce's tiny garlic cubes and wet basil bits up, then up in a direct flight to his mouth. Chewing he said —Babe. Babe, this sauce is amazing.

—I know.

—Plus it's like kicking my ass right now.

—I know. I know I think I'm really high already.

The clock made a bold but unfruitful pass at the hour, and outside, from a passing car, a scream dragged through the air, mangled and unintelligible.

—What was that?

—Kids.

—Kids?

—Kids, yeah.

—Kids. I don't want any kids. I don't know. My clock I think it's confused....

—So. I got a new one to pitch.

She smiled and her lips said —Perfect. Perfect timing. Awesome. Come on over here.

—Over where?

—Over here. We'll have some more Lancer's.

—Lancer's? Lancer's no, no, no Lancer's. No more Lancer's. I'm ripped.

—Come on. Just one glass. We'll share it.

—No.

—Baby?

—Fine, he said, and they got up unsteadily, hand in hand, one towing the other across the tobacco wood floor, to where the carpet raised a boundary, and stopped, stooped, struggled with shoes until unshod, to go nigh a tumbling for the couch upon which they plopped.

—Okay. Okay we're here.

—You forgot the Lancer's.

—Dammit...Baby?

—Don't look at me. I'm not going. Too full. Plus I don't want any anyway.

—Well I do dammit. I do. I'm going, she said, getting up, standing stalled a moment, then going. A walk with hips wrapped in a pencil skirt. He watched her feet negotiate scattered shoes, then the bump, bump, bump of her ass passed a wall where it disappeared. His gaze wandered to the window's drawn reed shades, through which he could not see, and then suddenly, a crash, glass, quick he swiveled his head back at the kitchen. —Dammit!

—What? he said, not moving.

—Fuck! Fuck no nothing. She sounded far. —Nothing. No nothing, it's all in the sink it broke in the sink. Don't worry. Dammit that was a good glass too don't worry it's nothing. And out she came, holding bottle and glass in one hand, the other far out to one side as if for balance, listing slightly to one side. She came across the carpet, where his eyes drew to the pink French-nailed toes. —Okay. Okay ready? she said, pouring at a tilt, setting the bottle down on the coffee table piled with *Wired*s, *Utne*s, *Nat Geo*s. —Sure you don't want any? she said, proffering the flute, sitting down on one leg folded underneath, the other's knee up close to her chin, her back on the armrest. She faced the side of his face, which had assumed a faraway look.

—No. I'm sure, he said.

—Okay. She maneuvered her fingers for a dainty grip.

—Okay, listen. Check it out. . .

—Wait.

—What?

—Does it have a name?

—No, not really. Not yet.

—Okay, shoot, she said, sipping, blinking, shifting.

—All right. Okay. Okay one, two, three eyes open your last decided day / set / stoned plus high on a colossal hit taken in your truck and abandoned in the parking lot where the search for you will surely begin / and prove fruitless / not found but missing / under the deep sea green sea fret mad with points of light dancing arhythmically on peaks of loud sun under which you bob / up, down, side to side heading outward / skiffwise / the no-motor sounds of the Evinrude sputters and stops / and you're floating adrift, far from a skyline gray and nameless. / Now, we see you, the third eye in / the beard's patchy mustaches don't quite meet under your nose / cheap rock star Ray-Ban replicas / you light a cigarette with difficulty in the wind / soundless labor only your windy hair tells us. / Cigarette dangles / shades up on forehead / you swivel three-sixty from shoulder to shoulder / through heavily hooded raccoon eyes / and smile, freer each minute. / Take up off the deck a blue labelless jug, pop its cap, then over portside pour its crimson bloom / and when it's empty it's flotsam, then another jug empty it's flotsam too. / Now sit. / Breathe. / Taste the air's salt. / Deep. Good. / Turn, undo the skiff's plug to unplugged, watch its inward flow. / Good. / Now, with the thirty-eight in your waistband / put five holes in the jugs and the deck at your feet. / Chucks spattered red and wet and sinking fast / felt good, the sound / to fire what you put in your mouth to press its barrel hot quick do it quick before you pussy out and... / you don't hear it, and we don't hear it / but your head snaps back and the implosion of halo blinds us. / Segue. / The show you never showed up at. / A gag gun resting on a blue velvet pillow / under podium glass / with its flag out unfurled in red it says: BANG. / Segue. / Forty-by-fifty-inch Duratran of her silhouette, waist up / in a beach's waves wearing a sun halo, in front of a crooked horizon of clouds too wispy to cast shadows / the water's mad sea fret's light points. / Segue. / Part Two of this grainy triptych. / This one of blustery Australian pines in the rain / through a beaded window. / Segue. / A plain lawn / trimmed square and lush enveloped in a night where Christmas lights are the only light. / Segue. / A film loop short of one Cuban melodious finch taking flight from a cupped hand / and your father's mustache smiling / and again the bird taking flight / and again the mustache smiling / and again, and again. / Segue. / Segue to nothing as your empty head's skull finds Truth / sinking with the sway of a falling leaf / flashing scenes filled with search and longing. / A church made outdoors of a swamp called Big Cypress / an earth shelter from a felled tree inspired by Wakan Tanka / asked of it, begged of it / gave found offerings as such at every meal / leftovers mud fights running naked some loin-clothed Mom would kill you if she found out / swamp on your face laughing at a horsefly alighting Chris's dick and birders you'd later strive to be spied you all hiding in tall grass / contemplating attack with mud balls / and at one's howling cue had them running terrified of the wild creature you became. / You made a gift of redly bloomed loins to a girl with silver eyes / came on a Mariel boatlift. / Jou gonna chair dat or watt? she said / to you and your bowl / until the day you woke in an abandoned house surrounded by many carpet puddles of Mad Dog and cherry-flavored, Cysco-colored vomit / and later she accosted you in Spanish with a spent rubber she pulled from her snatch after you'd lost it in there faking a no-orgasm. / You. / You see this. / A lady cop who once pulled you over and asked, You got a good throwing arm? / to which you answered, Y-yes. / She let you hurl the bowl into a strawberry field. / You'd search it the next day / after she'd made you park your truck at a church so she could drive you home. / First ride in

the back of a cop car, uncuffed. / Be more careful, she said. / And your
first hit now relived. / God, finally. / Under the watchful black eye of the
girl you loved and watched die. / Is this the end? / Scenes good and bad
now flash fleeting, unclassified. / It all flashes faster, faster, unbelievably
faster until through a darkness you hurtle toward a white sliver of light /
and there's an unfamiliar piping, almost squeaky sound in three, two,
one are you, are you asleep?

—No...No, my eyes, they were just closed. Your voice, it was kind of
hypnotic.

—Don't know if that's good or bad.

—No, no it's good I'm just gone. Were you making that up?

—Kind of. Not really.

—Baby, I'm tired. I don't think I can move.

—Come on, come on I got you, he said, and turned. He took the flute to
an uncluttered spot on the tabletop, then —Come on, up, up, he said and
upped and went and scooped one arm under her legs, the other under
her back. Her arm rounded his shoulders and he carried her easily across
the carpet and then the wood floor to a more thickly-piled bedroom
carpet. He lay her gently in the bed fully dressed, where she remained
watching as he turned and sat on the bed's edge, his back to her. Her
eyes closed, and when she opened them his form was still there, in the
same spot, as the room filled with slatted light leaking from blinds still
drawn.

—Babe. Babe, your phone is ringing.

—What? What, where?

—Your phone, it's ringing.

—What time is it?

—It's morning time.

—Oh shit. Jesus. Where is it?

—I'll get it...Here, he said.

—Oh...Hello...Hello, Mom...? Oh, no, hi, yes, yes this is she yes,
hi...Yes...yes, no God, I'm sorry, Mandy, yes...Yes, put her on...
Mom...Mom...Mom...Stop it, Mom, listen Mom no...No, Mom it's not
poison no one's trying to poison you, Mom. Mom, it's your medicine,

you have to take it...Mom, no, please stop, don't say that, it's not nice, Mom. They're hearing you please...They're not dykes, Mom, they're just trying to give you a bath. When was the last time you bathed?... Today? Just now? You always say that, just now...You always say that and it means you haven't bathed in God knows how long. I know you, Mom...Mom, no, yes. No, Mom, I'm coming over. Yes...Edward Mom Edward's been...Put Mandy on...Don't worry about Alex, Mom. Put Mandy on...Mom, no please don't start, put Mandy on. Mandy? Yes, Mandy. I'm sorry. I'm yes I'm coming over...No that's no problem yes thank you Mandy no... No, no, no Doctor Roig was by yesterday right...right... adjusted her meds yeah figures...No, no problem...Yes, thank you I'm...I'm on my way yes...Yes...Yes, goodbye. Baby, Baby, Baby, I need the bathroom whoa...

—All yours, he said, appearing suddenly in the bathroom doorway, planting a kiss so quickly she couldn't react. She looked at him smiling. Then she went in while he raided the kitchen nosily for Pom, toast, butter, jam. He spread it with a steak knife, left it stabbed in the seedy goo. He stood by the window over the sink's shattered good crystal, looking out at a mocking bird pair building a nest in the branch of a live oak outside, unseen in its entirety from his chewing vantage.

—Baby. Baby, you're at the butter again.

—I know. It's good.

—So much for austerity and cutting back and all that.

—So much, yeah. I have work to do.

—I have to go see my mom.

—Everything all right? Need me to come with?

—No. Yeah. Everything's all right. I guess they had to change her meds again and she's adjusting. She'll be fine. Better if I go alone.

He stood there chewing toast and then drank his juice and the clock stood poised for another pass at the hour. —You gonna eat something?

—I'm not hungry.

—Sure you don't want me to come with?

—Positive. Listen, next week's her birthday, remember? I want to cut her a cake there. We'll get everyone over.

—Oh yeah, for sure. That's sweet.

—Like last year was good. We'll sing Happy Birthday. And then she'll look at the cake and ask whose birthday it is, remember?

—Oh yeah. I got an idea for that come to think.

—What is it?

—We'll have to bring party hats to do it right, pass them around. We'll sing Happy Birthday, and then later, as soon as she asks whose birthday it is, we don't answer or explain anything but just burst into song again, all on cue, and sing the whole song again all the way through, everyone wearing party hats, and we do that every time she asks even if we have to sing Happy Birthday a hundred times that day. We'd have to tell everyone so they're prepared for it to work. Whadaya think?

—That's...That's fucking brilliant, her smile said, gigantically, with teeth, and she took his face in both hands and kissed it deeply in a block of sun.

—Okay, Baby. I'll be back later.

—All right, bye.

He stood there in the kitchen a while after the door slammed. Then he took to his poetry desk in the spare room and scribbled in spiral notebooks endless strings of words in a spider-scrawl script, unpunctuated with a black Pilot until suddenly he stopped mid-thought, mid-word even, and rested his chin in his hand, gazing out the window, not really seeing how the clouds moved with the cat claw's leaves, or how the sky's colors changed as the sun arced, dialing shadows of homes, cars, trees, light poles spired like clocks while inside window shadows painted slowly up and down the walls and the floors and the clock made several unreciprocated passes at the hour.

—Baby! Baby you hungry?!

—Huh! Who's there?!

—I said you hungry Baby it's me! I stopped and picked up some Chinese!

—Thank God. Fuck. I'm starved.

—Fried dumplings. What?! Braised tofu in black bean sauce and rice, special fried rice and I got us a bag of those fortune cookies you like!

—Babe! Babe, I got a new one to pitch! Come in here!

—Awesome but, but can it wait til after we eat?!

—No, no it's really short. Come in here!

She came, stood in the doorway.

He swiveled his chair to face her. —Ready?

—Shoot.

—AAAAAAAAAAGHHHHHHHHH!

—Dude...

—AAAAAAAAAAAGGGGHHHHH!

—Dude!

—AAAAAAAAAAAAAAGGGGGGGGGGGGGGHHHHHHHHH!

—Dude, stop that!

—AAAAAAAGGGGH, AAAAAAAAAAAAAAAAAGGGHHH!

—Bay...

—AAAAAGGGHH!

—....

—AAAAAAAAAAAAAGGGHH!...

—Are you done?

—Ahm. Ahm, yes.

—That was bad. I mean, really bad.

—What?

—Not good, baby.

—Really? You don't think?

—Baby.

—It's called The Screamer.

—I don't think I get it.

—Me neither. Let's eat.

—I think the neighbors probably heard that, she said, as they picked with chopsticks at food out of little white oriental cartons standing in the kitchen. Soon the door knocked.

—I'll get it, he said.

—I think I know who it is, she said, part of a dumpling occluding her words.

—Hey, he said.

It was Al, their downstairs neighbor. He had one hand behind his back. He said —Hi, um, I'm sorry, don't mean to bother but, but is everything all right up here?

—Yeah, yeah why do you ask?

—I thought I heard someone screaming.

—I told you! she said, from the kitchen, still dumpling-occluded.

—Oh yeah no. No that was just me just, just fucking around you know.

—Oh, said Al.

—Thanks for coming up to check, though. That's real nice of you, dude. Dude, what's that you got behind your back? Is that a gun?

—Can't ever be too safe, bub. Know what I mean?

—Well...Yeah well...I guess it's kind of scary, though.

—What you mean the gun?

—No, just guns in general.

—For home safety and protection only, bub. Nothing to worry about.

—I guess. I guess, I think. It's good to know, though, that you're down there with that like...like Rambo.

—Ha ha. Funny. You should quit screaming like that. Sounded like someone getting killed.

—My bad.

—All right, bub. I'm going.

—All right. Okay. Thanks, though, I'm serious, he said as Al walked off downstairs, not responding. Then he quietly closed the door and came back into the kitchen.

—I told you, she said. —See, I told you.

—Told me what? he said, chop sticking a flap of tofu.

—That awful screaming. Not good, Baby.

—He had a gun.

—We're lucky he didn't call the cops.

—I couldn't see it, though. He had it behind his back.

—That was really nice of him. I mean, it's odd but...but you know, nice.

—Yeah. This tofu's great. Really. Did you have some?

—Yes, but these dumplings. Mmm.

—How's your mom, by the way?

—She's fine, I guess. In fucking la la land. Keeps talking about stuff that happened years ago as if it happened yesterday. Everyone who's dead is alive again. I haven't the heart to tell her they're dead, so I end up making up stories about what they're doing now. I leave feeling like I'm losing my mind too. She thinks you're this loser Larry I dated in college.
—That's funny. Last year I was that coke dealer you dated, remember? She wouldn't talk to me.
—Yeah, no, but you know what is funny is I was thinking on my way home how I used to think it was Old Timer's.
—Old Timer's?
—Yeah.
—Well, it kinda sounds like Alzheimer's.
—No but I think I thought that up until I was like twenty-two or something.
—Oh. Oh yeah, that's retarded.
—Dumbass, huh?
—Kind of.
—You know that was really nice of Al coming up to check on us like that. I wanted to say something but the dumplings had my mouth hostage. I haven't eaten all day. It looked for a second like the clock finally had something going with the hour but no. —I feel like I should go say thanks, take him some brownies or something.
—Take him some butter. He ranted about it last time I gave him some. Or maybe take him that pesto you made.
—Really, he smokes?
—I don't know but he liked the butter, came up an hour later all gushing about it, you.
—Yeah. Yeah maybe I'll take him some now before it gets too late, you think? she said, setting the carton down and chopsticks crosswise on top of it. She went and leaned deep into the fridge's light for a Tupperware and then came out and up for a clean Tupperware from the cupboard to place in it a neat stack of brownies and a stick of butter on the side. — Hell, he can have the rest of this pesto too, huh? holding both containers out to both sides in front of the fridge like a game show model.

—You're a sweetheart.

By the time the door slammed he'd demolished the tofu. His phone rang as he passed it on the dining table's Yugoslavian wood and picked it up not answering it until he'd plopped into his thinking chair. —Hello... Hey yeah yo what's up?...Yeah...Yeah...Yeah you mean the one with the lips and fake tits you met on Facebook, the one who at the slightest touch of your just-average penis screams so loud at night in your apartment she wakes your neighbors up like houses down the street, the one your landlord's one-hundred-and-eight-year-old deaf mother thinks is cats fighting, and who your landlord himself calls the screamer, jovially in spite of your utter embarrassment, the girl I now hear you've abandoned at different venues in unsuccessful attempts at getting her pissed off so you can finally start a fight with her and quote unquote break up with her already, but who hasn't said one thing about such calculatingly cold and atrocious behavior on your part, dude. Dude, is all that true...? Hello...? Hello...?

—Hello?

—Hello?

—Hello...? Hello...? Hello can you hear me...? Yeah, yeah I think the lines got crossed...Yeah that was her I think I'm not tryin'a answer...Left her at The Bar just now yeah...Yeah, it's true...Yeah, bro, seriously infuckingcredible. I've left her at the Abbey, Fox's, The Seven Seas Sunset Tavern and a bunch'a other places I can't remember now and nothing, not a peep as I up and excuse myself to the bathroom but instead leave out the back, go home with my phone off until the next day she calls and she's like Hey? What's up? Where are you? What're we doing tonight? As if nothing odd'd happened the night prior and I have no clue how she ever even gets home, bro...Yeah, probably a taxi...? Brutal...? No you know what's brutal is now I find out she's got two kids and one of em's autistic...Yeah...Yeah and the screaming bro I can't take it...Yeah, hot as hell or no yeah she is but dumb as hell too, bro, and really, man, that screaming, that screaming's a turn-off I can't take it embarrassing me in front of my neighbors my landlord dude never heard anything like it bro I'm serious says she's coming the whole time...A disease?...No...No... No...Wow. I never heard'a that...Really?...Wow...Oh, wow...Wow, sounds like it now come to think...Incredible yeah it's really not that hard to believe...Looks painful shit it sounds painful lemme tell you... Yeah she says she's coming the whole time and like I'm like bathed in pussy juice me the bed and her all three we get like sluiced. When we're done. Done, yeah, yeah and she shakes shakes no convulses, bro, and pants...Like a dog like she needs CPR yeah wow...Disease, huh?...Well yeah disease or no she's got one fucking sure mental disease who'd get stood up like that and not say anything?...Plus yeah she likes it rough, she says, and get this last one she pulled fucking disease *please*...Yeah no listen I can't take it anymore dude listen... No seriously listen...Listen I took her to Fox's planning to dump her there again when Brian and Ryan and Jorge show up all drunk already. Apparently Jorge'd managed to get them all kicked outta Sunset Tavern after brutalizing some poor college kid probably and now here they were barging in on my quote date with Melissa, Jorge openly ogling her tits bursting from her blouse and I'm like Guys, don't you got somewhere to go? And Jorge's like Yeah, we're going to BT's...Yeah... The strip club...Yes...Yes...Yes, dude...I don't know bro listen... Yeah...Yeah...Yeah so at the word BT's her eyes light up and she's like Oh I wanna go and I'm like No, you don't, and she's like Yes, I do, and I'm like No, you don't, but she did and was adamant and we went and then get this she ends up getting a lap dance from some equally-busted stripper there and then actually gets up on stage and strips herself...Yes...Yes, she actually stripped at the club, for everyone, Jorge and Brian cheering and gently placing dollar bills she took sensually between her tits squishing them together with her hands...I shit you not, bro, and I'm sitting there with Ryan going Dude, where the hell'd you find this chick? I told him the Internet...Snot funny, bro...I can't...Because I tried and she cried and then introduced me to her kids so I felt bad, ended up fucking her doggie-style in the bathroom while she bit and yelled into a towel still on the rack so her kids wouldn't hear...What? try your what trick?...Mask trick?... Did you say mask trick what the...? Yeah...Yeah...Wow...Wow yeah that's good...That's really good, bro. You still got it?...Yeah... Great yeah can I come get it?...Get when now hold on no...Yeah I'll come over no hold on no...Hello...? Hello...?

—Hello...?

—Hello...?

—Hello...? Hello...? Hello? Can you hear me? Yeah I think something's wrong with your phone, dude...No...Yeah, sure I'll be here.

The door swung open and —Dude Al's really a nice guy I had no cl...oops, my bad.

—Yeah, man...Yeah, man, whenever...Sure thing, all right...later.

—Who was that?

—Diego.

—Diego? Jeez, I can't believe him.

—What?

—Dumping that girl at bars.

—How do you know about that anyway?

—Spoken to witnesses: Anne, Stephanie, Frank. They've seen him do it.

—Yeah, he was just telling me about it.

—How can anything be worse than bringing a girl to a bar, having a drink with her and then saying you're going to the bathroom but then slipping out the back instead? They've all seen him do it. It's no secret, and more than once. I hear she just finishes her drink there all nonchalant and then calls a cab. What can be worse than that? Tell me what? You said you've seen worse but tell me. She sat on the couch next to his chair and reached for the coffee table's cigar box. —Please tell me.

—Okay. I knew this guy in college, had a problem with a girl, a really clingy girl who took no no's for an answer, made breaking up impossible. So he was inspired one day he says to buy a mask, a really lurid mask of an old man that covered half his face from the nose up. It was bald and liver-spotted on the crown's rubbery skin, a flappy-type mask with wiry white tufts of hair skirting the temples and over the ears, the nose an ugly bulbous thing complete with warts, high ruddy puffy cheeks and wrinkles. A horrid thing, really, in its realness, meaning on him it looked fucking real. So he walked out the costume shop wearing it. Then, at home, he put some cheap yellow heart-shaped sunglasses without lenses on it, stuck in the hair over his real ears, only those and his real chin and mouth exposed. He hides the mask in the nightstand drawer and when he brings her home after a night out rattling bars, they have sex doggie-style and without her noticing he dons the mask, starts pulling her hair, slapping her ass, calling her bitch, slut, whore, rag until she turns and sees the mask and tries to buck, but he holds tighter until she cries out *please stop* and he lets go, steps back and starts to jack off looking at her through the eyehole's heart shapes, not saying anything, just standing there. She asks him to please stop, he's scaring her. But he doesn't. He keeps masturbating, standing there. She says stop it please, take me home, and he says take a cab, I'm not done here...

—Stop it, you can't be serious.
—Fine.
—Would you like oop, a knock. —I wonder who that is?
—It's Diego.
—Diego?
He was at the door, opening it. —Hey, man. Come in.
—Hey, thanks.
—Hold up, I'll go get it.
—Hi, Diego.
—Hi, Laura.
—Would you like?
—No, no thanks. I really gotta run.
—So what brings you?
—Picking something up. Just...I was in the neighborhood.
—Here.
—What's in the bag?
—Something.
—Whoa. Wicked. Wow.
She looks down into the bag. —Oh my god. You were serious?
—This thing is wicked, bro.
—That was you?
She shakes her head, mouth open.
—Tried to tell you.
—All right, bro...Well, thanks.
—Sure thing, man. Let me know how it works.

—Yeah. Later.
The door is softly closed.
—I can't...I can't believe it.
—What?
—That...You.
He comes to her.
—Stop it.
—What?
—That...Please.
—Oh...Ooh...

Are You Okay?

I can hear them talking. I can hear them making noise out in the front yard and throughout the house. I'm alone in this room, trying to hear a record. But it's a record I have, and I've heard it lots of times, and but then the sounds coming out aren't the sounds of that record.

I watch the needle on the vinyl spin til it starts to skip around the sticker. I let it skip. I let it skip...

Then I feel someone standing behind me.

I don't turn right away, but no one says anything, so I turn.

I've never seen her before. She's not wearing anything. She's standing there naked with her feet close together on the carpet. She has strawberry hair, and when she speaks her lips hardly move, and she weaves tiny meaningless things in the air with her hands at her sides.

She goes, Do you have...are you...are you the guy they call Dude With The Hair?

Yeah, I go.

The record skips.

And she goes, Do you have...can I have a hit or...or a roll just...just one, I mean.

You mean just one of each? I go.

And she goes, Yeah.

She takes only two steps closer to take them from my hand, and then her feet come close together again. She has impeccable posture. Her navel is level with my sitting eyes staring into it. A scar. A tapered little hole it seems endless, black in its deepest part.

I give her one and one.

She goes, I don't have any money but...but we can have sex, if you want.

I look at her. The record skips.

She doesn't take either one, just holds them in her hand. Then she goes and sits on the stripped bed and lies back.

I watch her. The record skips. The kids outside make noise and loud-talk, and a bottle breaks on asphalt, and someone screams. In through the window comes a breeze, smells of dew, and night, and her skin is a pale white and it reflects the shine and the vascular colors of the flowers and the leaves on the mattress. It takes her shape.

I undo my belt and jean buttons. She opens her legs to me.

I do this thing where I count thrusts in my head. It's not a linear count but odd in the way that I just say random numbers to forty, or twelve, or seventeen or whatever and then start over, and not necessarily at one. I don't know why I do this. I count slowly, watching her.

Her eyes are green. They're perfectly normal, average, a beautiful solid green that looks not into mine but up past them and through the back of my skull at the ceiling. She doesn't make a sound.

I feel myself go, and I pull out, getting up off the bed, letting go all on Dante's stripped mattress, and then on the carpet.

I stand doing my pants and belt. She stays lying there.

The record skips.

I go, Are you okay?

And she goes, Yeah.

And I go, Okay. I'm leaving.

And she goes, Okay. Bye.

Then I leave that room downstairs past kids there clutching beer bottles close to their bodies. They make words I understand not one of. Their faces are dark. Their grins are like fixtures and they make dental drill sounds as I go through and out of the house, and then across the lawn, despite someone calling maybe my name back like, Yo hey where you going, Dude!? But I know not where, down streets in the dark, by a lake, then another, and a dog watches me cross a street too late to have cars on it. I walk west til the sun casts its sticky light over me and the tops of the houses and the trees and the sounds of traffic rise, and I stop at the coming of a yellow Volkswagen bus with dark tints. It pulls up right next to me. The driver's side window comes down and out pours white smoke and Levi's blond-framed face emerges going, Dude! Get in.

I go around to the other side where the suicide doors open and take me in, and I find a couch to sit on. There are lots of people in here, but I can't see what happens, and in another lapse I find myself at a party in someone's house where everybody's in swim trunks or bikinis or some other thing for wet fun and loud sun and here splashes a pool the whole time. I get a blowjob in the bathroom, looking at myself and the back of her head in the mirror, propped against a towel rack. When she comes up I ask her is she okay and she says yeah, she's fine. I'm not sure what I give her. Something.

Soon I find myself ushered into a car. It's night.

Have I slept?

I may have said that out loud.

I don't know these guys save for the one driving: Kenny? I know him from...*school*? He says they need me at a party in Pinecrest, but he's on his way there already, driving like it's an emergency.

Up in the passenger seat a kid with a giant brown afro like the Happy Trees Guy complete in a polyester flared collar keeps putting the volume higher because he can't hear. It's really loud in the back where I'm at with this kid sporting a mischievous greaser mustache and floppy hair. He has in his hand a lighter he keeps flicking to show me the spark in the dark, and some headlights pass flashing a smile on his face, and then he reaches the lighter to the kid in the front's afro and flicks its spark and a flame comes up and up the afro goes in a big ball of fire. The whole car lights up inside. And the kid complains loudly and beats his own head with his hands going Fuck! Fuck, dude, fuck. What the fuck!

But now we're all laughing uncontrollably, even the kid whose afro's all burnt lopsided, and Kenny keeps going: the smell, the smell and Jesus, and we're all laughing and can't stop laughing when the kid with the stache next to me puts the lighter away in his pocket and starts fondling the door handle. But then all of a sudden something happens where real quick the door opens and he falls out and the door shuts behind him and he's gone. Just like that.

I start to laugh harder. I slap my leg. It was like a magic trick or special effect or something, and my laughs make Kenny and the half-burnt afro kid laugh even harder. Kenny's trying hard to not swerve.

It takes Kenny one, two, three quick looks over his shoulder to put the volume down and go Dude! Dude, where's Danny?

Are you asking me? I go.

The kid with the afro's face has trouble seeing back around the afro's new shape.

Well...Well, yeah, Dude, you're back there, goes Kenny.

And I'm like, I don't know, dude. Dude just opened the door and got out.

Then Kenny goes, Whadaya mean? Whadaya mean he got out? We haven't stopped!

I said I don't know, dude. He just opened the door and left, I go.

And the burnt Afro kid goes, He didn't like, like say anything before he left?

Uh, no, I go and Kenny's goes, Fuck. Fuck, Jesus, Fuck. Fuck. And he says that all the way to some big house in Pinecrest.

In the kitchen things fly out of my pockets into the hands and mouths of others as I partake in bong hits compliments of the people there. Again I can't understand anything anyone says. Their faces are dark, and the fixtures fry, and I notice a girl with black hair and black eyes look at me sideways, smiling and then laughing at something someone said, and in another lapse the doorbell rings.

I don't know how exactly, but I somehow know who. Someone goes and opens the door, and yeah, it's Danny. He's got a Pizza Hut pizza box, holding it up like a waiter, and his hair is tousled with sticks and leaves in it. His face is all scratched. A bloody road burned shoulder shows through a tear in his T-shirt. He steps inside, and for a minute no one says anything, so he goes: Uh, got this pizza here from some dude out there. Ate a slice on the way. Got hungry, you know. It's Hawaiian.

Then here comes Kenny and the Asymmetrical Afro Kid, asking him questions with words that meet, mix, tangle, mangle to nothing understandable, so I leave and find a room alone with a record player in it. I find the same record I was trying to hear at Dante's and put it on, and but then the same thing happens til the needle on the arm on the vinyl starts to skip around the sticker in the middle, and I conclude something's gone seriously wrong.

I let it skip...

Then I feel someone standing behind me.

I don't turn right away, but no one says anything, so I turn.

It's the girl with the sideways smile and the black hair and the black eyes from the kitchen. Very pretty. Impeccable posture. She's not wearing anything. She stands with her feet close together on the carpet.

She goes, I know about you.

I don't say anything. The record skips.

And she goes, Do you wanna have sex?

I nod.

We do it on the bed. This one's got sheets, made. She makes breathy noises looking up through the back of my skull at the ceiling as I count nonlinear thrusts in my head. Her eyes are black holes, all pupil, and I pull out and let go all on the bed between her legs, and what gets on the inside of her thigh she wipes off with a thumb onto the sheets, and smiles. She has big even white teeth and her almost brown nipples are the shape and hardness and thickness of dimes.

She says something I can't hear.

I get dressed. She stays lying there.

Are you okay?

Her mouth goes Yeah, but I can't hear anything but *shhhhk, shhhhk, shhhhk...*

Okay, I go. I'm leaving.

And her mouth goes Okay. Bye.

Then I leave that room through the house's dark-faced people, grinning out into the night, where the streets newly wet shine under lamps and the hiss of passing cars. Killdeers call their name in the dark of the night in the air, unseen, and I walk til the shadow of my head appears on the street, up ahead, on the road, but really, really far out.

The Boy Who Wanted to Make Things Fall Up

He studied physics, thermodynamics, math, dark forces, the Occult. Once he got a maple leaf to crawl across his desk. Another time he got a matchbook to hover inches from his palm. After that, everyday magic tricks got boring; only so much could a kid do with handkerchiefs and top hats, knotted scarves, doves and bunnies.

He was a round-faced boy. He grew into a round-faced, double-chinned, doughy man, a magician who lost control of his powers and, in turn, countless sets of keys, money, food...sandwiches, spare change, key rings with all his keys on them soaring into the sky fast as the eye could see, into the atmosphere, space, and beyond.

Visit him in his home.

See everything he's touched.

Everything stuck to the ceiling to never again come down.

Jackson Crisis and Detox

I remember this one fucking time I did sorta that. Jeez. I'd picked up a one-n-one you know, one boy and one girl, from the same trap hole or whatever you wanna call it in the Hood on my way home from work. Mind I wasn't deep into another habit or anything then. I wasn't even chipping. It was just a one-time thing this. You know. This one time among many one times.

Okay, yeah, go ahead and laugh but it's true: Once I'm off I'm off, and if I'm on I'm on, and if I'm chipping, well, I'm still on but with a shitty or nonexistent cash flow, soon to be off again, is the thing.

But none'a that was the case. I was off. I had a job, an apartment, even a girl, and a good one too, a smart one, meaning she had the sense to leave once she really got to know me. But anyway. I copped a one-n-one plus a seta works and went home, this little pad I had on northeast second and twenty-second, the railroad tracks not even a whole block away at the end of the cul-de-sac.

But wait. I think I have to explain a little the goings-on around this place before I go on for this to make any sense because listen, while at this pad I'd had more than a few encounters with drunk crackhead homeless types. Like get this: Evie and I came home from a club one night rolling and a bit drunk to find this big tall black linebacker-like dude with a nappy beard that Evie would later refer to as The Big Homeless Crack Monster on my front porch smoking crack in a stem. I lived in Apartment One, and there he was, not even really hiding or even trying to but just there by my door sitting cross-legged on the floor. There was like visible dumpster detritus all stuck in his beard which for all I knew looked to be growing honest dreads like newborn tentacles and Evie and I'd stopped short of seeing him and she like inched around behind me. Remember now that we were on X, and it was at this point that I addressed him, at the same time reaching for my jeans ass pocket I was like, Uh, excuse me but what the fuck are you doing? But he didn't say anything right away because he'd apparently just taken a blast he was still holding and probably just beginning to fly from and so we waited a few seconds, only steps between us and The Big Homeless Crack Monster, still sitting there with his charred stem and cheap lighter. But then he blew out the smoke and said, Just one minute please. I could almost hear Evie blink in disbelief behind me. I was like *Please*? Dude there ain't no fucking please about this: Get the fuck outta here before I call the cops, I said. This was the E talking probably because had I been just a wee bit more drunk it woulda been the drunk talking and saying nothing but one'a those potted plants out there upside his head. But lucky I was rolling, because then I brandished my phone as I would've a gun had I had one, only pointing it at my own head instead. He said, No need for that, no need and up and walked off past us gigantically down the street, his rags flapping, disappearing into the night as we watched just sorta stuck there.

And that was just one instance. This other time in the morning real early I got up for work at the Midtown Mall site we were building there on Northeast Second and Thirty-Fifth but whatever I got in my truck and turned it on and was about to drive when I smelled it. It was that rotting drunk wino vomit smell. You know it. You smell it everywhere Downtown all the time. So I look over my shoulder into the backseat and there he was gravely asleep and bearded like Jesus entombed. It took lotsa screaming and jabbing with my police lock and shaking the truck from the outside to get him up and the fuck outta there and weeks, literally fucking *weeks* to get the lingering dry vomit smell to go away.

Shit I could go on with these instances. I lived in that place almost two years and these encounters were an at least once a month occurrence. But anyway my point is I was already in the back of my mind always paranoid living there coming home every day, especially at night, the result of gentrification I guess. It got so bad that whenever Evie and I came home late from anywhere she walked behind me like prodding me along and no way would she ever walk from her car alone at night to my apartment door but instead she'd call from outside down the street and I'd go out to wait for her.

So anyway this day it was night, but not that late, and I was subconsciously paranoid, coming home with the gear...You get what I mean by subconsciously paranoid right?

"Right."

Okay, so I come in all giddy for my one time fix getting my head blown to bits, and even though I'm right to it not even locking the door or anything and throbbing with the anticipation so that I could almost taste it already I'm doing this whole routine or like ritual very slowly and deliberately. I had a couch I sat on in front of the TV and a sorta like makeshift milk crate coffee table with an old Red Krayola record sleeve taped to it like a top between and there I sat on the couch with my rig, the gear, the demitasse with water I got on my way in through the kitchen along with a spoon. But now I was never really into speedballs so I'm doing my dope separately — girl first, boy later and as you probably know a DP in OT's pretty much always good for two or more blasts I'm ready to have my own little personal party with before Evie calls wanting to go out and drink or dance or something or whatever and so I'm there with the little yellow baggie between my thumb and bird finger tapping with the index trying to get half the flake out. It was one solid chunk in there and didn't wanna break and I'm struggling, getting nervous for no reason but then all of a sudden it comes out the whole fucking thing like plop into the spoon. Well most of it at least. What was left in the bag was pointless, like enough residue for a good taste. And now I'm looking at this shit thinking it's *really* good shit — scaly, yellowish-white shiny oily shit. And the rock's huge, like way too much I'm thinking. So I look at the baggie, what's in it: Pointless. But what happens next is like a reverse confusion: Pointless to do what's left alone in one shot, not thinking that maybe I should try and put half back in the baggie and plus I'm like fuck it: One Time, One Time Huge Blast For Old Time's Sake or some shit my mind says and I'm pouring the pointless residue out into the spoon like dusting the big-enough-to-kill boulder and I'm shaking I'm so excited, drawing some water from the demitasse, about a whole barrelful, and then squirting it down onto the mini ghetto coke mountain in my spoon watching it dissolve like, not like butter, but like some really good oily shit you could see it swirling in the spoon's water, the oil...Shit. My bad. I can see you're like sweating and slightly shaking over there. Me talking about this.

"Yeah. No. No worries. I'm always like this, here. Go on."

Okay, so I draw this like syrup into the rig and set it down on the coffee table there with its empty bag and the boy and the spoon and the little cup with the water, the dark-eyed chick in the organdy bra with the Super-8 on the sleeve staring sexily up at me tying off with my belt my left arm I'm thinking, *Jesus*, just looking at the rig. The goo was yellow. Straight up. The hell was I thinking? But I was like fuck it, right, I've already come this far. So I spiked a vein, found the rose, sent it home and then BOOOOSHHHH I mean really. My ears fucking screamed and I didn't just taste it in my mouth but exuded that shit out every pore like I'd bathed in coke and ether, the apartment rolling around the couch affixed to the floor somehow upon the ceiling and I'm like okay, big mistake, stop this train whenever and I can't hear shit besides that white noisy cardiovascular roar. You know it. Killer, yeah, but too much really. I wasn't thinking about my heart just yet, or whether or not I was even breathing dude is that drool?

"No. Yeah. Continue."

Okay. So I'm poised not hearing still in this robotic tableau, the TV, that is, was on, but on mute and but I could still hear all the people in this little like faraway now box, all roboticking out, those crazy coke sounds, you know, a different animal mainline that shit is. And so I'm poised over the demitasse's water with the rig thinking I'll rinse it, one of the first of the twenty thousand wired things I'd do that night before Evie shows up, when I hear a bump in the closet. It was like *thump*, *kthump*. I'm like oh shit, bum in the closet, sleeping, waking up now. Perfect timing, huh?

"Holy shit are you serious?"

No, but I don't move, thinking intruder, burglar, stay calm. So I try and stay calm, but I'm wired as fuck. I mean beyond. Imagine, just. So out loud I say Pal, better find your way the fuck outta here before I hack you to pieces! I got a machete under the couch. But I don't say that, obviously. Actually, I might not have said anything at all probably wired as I was beyond any hint of verbal faculty. But that's when I hear the metallic slide and click of my dad's Remington twenty-gauge. I'd borrowed it from him that week, took Evie out shooting — skeet, bottles-n-shit — out in Homestead. Anyway, I hear it. And I freak. I stand and turn and flip the couch up onto the closet door. But that wasn't enough so I go and do the bed too, frame, box spring and all. Then a flimsy folding chair and this little wooden desk I had. All this shit's piled up on the closet door. It was a walk-in sorta closet so dude had plenty of room to do in there whatever he was doing. I'm nearly shitting myself now but wired as hell too so I grab the machete off the carpet where the couch was just at and like jump over the nightstand to hide behind it, taking cover like, like waiting for the shotgun blast to blast out through the couch and the bed's innards spraying springs flying everywhere I could hear it, see it happening all the while with the white cardiovascular noise whooshing through my head flying on the coke I was gripping the machete, sweating balls and trying hard to concentrate on breathing and not throwing up. That's when I thought about my heart. It felt super slow in my chest but pounding hard like BOOM...BOOM and for a second I thought I'd die, for good this time. It was so much in me but this whole scene was not fun. Not at all. It was a great beyond orgasmic rush but at such a horrible time.

　　Next thing you know I hear a voice like Oscar, it's the police, we're coming in, be calm. And it sorta jarred me, the voice, saying that, no longer sounding robotic. I was crouched behind the nightstand, my cellphone in my other hand. It was like a lapse. I couldn't remember ever even picking the phone up. But anyway I dropped the machete, and then the phone. Holy shit I was like what? Then I stood up with my hands in the air, my belt dangling off my biceps, blood all up my forearm, sweating like crazy. And they just stood there inside my apartment, which looked like someone huge had up and shaken it. The two goateed cops, former high school jocks surely, their side arms holstered stood expressionless like they'd seen this shit a million times. They told me I could put my hands down, but I didn't. Not for a while. They didn't bother searching me or my place or anything. They asked me questions but I couldn't hear clearly past the fuzz that for some reason seemed to be coming back now and I said I didn't know to everything they asked. I don't know, and that I was sorry. Sorry in every sense'a the fucking word. They didn't cuff me, didn't even touch me really. They gave me a ride in the back of the cop car to here and then left me to check in voluntarily if I wanted. Somehow I was already inside. Downstairs in the intake lobby I felt like a microwave oven, hot but cold and buzzing I read forms without seeing them, listened to the empty faces that reflected my thoughts, watched an orderly's black silent moving mouth make oval shapes as I said things about a fictitious and meaningless existence and scribbled enigmatic symbols on paper. The lady downstairs, the intake nurse, the same lady who's probably down there right now said, Sure you don't wanna stay the night? Relax? Recover? No thanks, I'm like. It was an accident, I go, perhaps referring to my life, or having survived this long. But she let me go anyway. I wouldn't dare get on a bus or a train or a mover. I walked straight from here to my apartment, straight through the Hood like I owned the place, hood rats and old schools hollering did I need something: boy, hards, *mantega* the way they say it at every corner. It was late, my ears like a rung bell still everything all fucking robosounds. Tremendous fucking blast that was. The hell was I thinking? But there wasn't anything in my mind at that point, not a thought the whole walk actually. I'm serious. Weirdly at peace like if nothing was left but.

When I walked through my apartment door, which had been left wide open, I started laughing. What a state! My pad looked...I don't even know. Total fucking mess. Everything all flipped up onto the closet door piled on with the intruder-burglar still inside. Ha. Then, laughing still, I set about looking for that little bag of dope I knew was still around someplace so I could finally go and what was that med-call? Did she just say med-call? Dude, let's go.

The Punkrocker's Girlfriend

He was singing aloud a song by Stephin Merritt, a songwriter he really, really liked, like liked A LOT, when she socked him in the face with a pillow. He liked to sing aloud, and he sang aloud well — a bold deep voice, a practiced baritone, dipping always lower and lower, so low it droned, almost like a bass. He was never fazed by anything when he sang and stopped only when the pillow rammed the cigarette deep into his mouth, its butt catching the back of his throat. It was a rich thick voice that all of a sudden stopped and lapsed into a coughing fit that expelled the cigarette like a comet from his mouth while a party of dispossessed rabid children with bats fashioned from broken tree branches paraded through the street outside whacking trashcans and mailboxes, goateed men in bowler hats chasing them with billy clubs.

When he finished coughing he went on singing. The rabid children had been at it for hours. It was as though they were running circles around their block. A car peeled out somewhere and something wet splashed like a water balloon. After a while he stopped singing and reached for another cigarette from his shirt pocket. She stood there. Then, all of a sudden, like a malfunction, she blinked like a million times really, really fast. Her eye shadow was yellow. It looked gross and gaudy to him now as her lids flickered up and down over her super-red eyes.

He stared at her.

"What the hell's wrong with you?" he said.

She nodded and brought her hand up and touched her fingers to the plastic arrow that appeared to pierce her skull. Tomorrow would be Sunday, her field trip day for the octogenarians at the Woodlawn Home. He kept looking at her, scratching his crotch, at the same time rubbing the side of his face where part of the cherry had caught him. She had milk-and-coffee skin and big straight white teeth in her mouth; the teeth, she insisted to friends, were her father's, who was Puerto Rican.

Then: "Hey Oscar, we got any'a those chocolate mushroom chunk pot brownies left? I want one."

He made a face like *Aw fuck*, because he wanted to sing another song, maybe, or maybe go to sleep, he couldn't decide. But her eyes freaked him out, watching him.

"Why don't you go to sleep, Estrella?" he said, annoyed. "You haven't slept in days."

"I'd like something for my mind first," she said. "My skull hurts for some reason, and I'm hungry."

He groaned extravagantly as he went out the door.

He opened the fridge and grabbed a brownie off the tray and brought it to her in his filthy upturned palm. She stood up straight and mock-saluted him when he came into the bedroom, then swung at him with the pillow and quickly lunged for the brownie, catching it midair when he dropped it employing a snazzy evasive maneuver. He thought she looked like a mental patient in her white smock. She took a tiny bite of brownie with the tips of her long straight teeth.

"What a funny little notion I had," she said.

"Shut the hell up," he said, getting into bed and turning over onto his side away from her. She's starting again, he thought, staring at the wall. Then he closed his eyes.

"What? You don't want to hear the notion I had?" she said.

"No," he said at the wall.

She came and sat on the edge of the bed and took another tiny bite of brownie. She chewed silently, then swallowed.

"Well, it was kind of a what-if notion, you know, with all kinds of complexly imagined relations going on. I dunno. It interested me when I had it. How long have we been awake, Oscar? It doesn't really matter, I guess. Anyway. Imagine we're hanging out someplace one night. I dunno where. But no friends, just the two of us. At a little far-out club or bar or something. Somewhere not familiar. And there's another, older couple there, and they want to take us for a ride on their scooter." She laughed, herself imagining it. "And we go and look at this scooter thing on the sidewalk outside the bar. Only the way it turns out the scooter's just got one seat big enough for three. You and I start arguing over who's gonna sacrifice and squeeze into the little basket thing mounted on the scooter's handlebar thing. You say you are, and I say I am. But finally I just jump up in there and squeeze in. It's so small my butt hurts, and I'm afraid if we crash or something like that I'm gonna get the worst of it. Would you let me?"

"That's some fucking notion, Estrella," he said at the wall. "You know Jessenia? Hugo's girlfriend? Well, she has notions that actually make fucking sense."

She looked at the brownie in her hand and took another bite. When she had swallowed, she wiped her free hand on the white comforter, leaving a big chocolate arc. Then she smiled, a little black smudge on one tooth.

"Do you remember that time we drove up to Lake Okeechobee, Oscar? At Fish Eating Creek? When you lost all our pot?" She placed her hand on his hip. "Do you remember that?" she said.

She did. It all of a sudden came up for some reason. She didn't know why. It was a month or two after they'd hooked up and gone away for a weekend. They had sat by a little campfire at night, a papaya in the sweet water-warm river, and she'd re-fried refried beans and grilled arepas and bacon for dinner and bacon and eggs and Cuban bread toasted in the same blackened pan the next morning. She had burned the pan both times she cooked, and they burned the coffee too, but it was one of the best times they'd ever had. She remembered he'd sung aloud to her that day as well: a Raymond Carver poem, or was it a story? She couldn't remember. He used to memorize whole stories and poems and sing them aloud to her. He used to be able to sing them both to sleep. They had slept out under the stars on top of their sleeping bags. It was the beginning of winter and there were no bugs. The next morning he lost their pot and somehow convinced other fellow campers around to help them find it.

"Well? Do you remember or not?" she said, patting him on the hip. "Oscar?"

"I remember," he said. He turned around and sat up, looked at her. He didn't remember very well, he thought. What he did remember were sculpted mohawks and cool ideas about music and recording and independent distribution on his record label, and he did not want to remember that.

"But who gives a shit anymore, Estrella?" he said.

"It was right before we dropped out of college to go on tour with your band," she said.

He waited, and then he scooted over to the edge of the bed and pulled her with him. "You about done with that brownie, Estrella?" She held it up and looked at it. She nodded. He took it and threw it hard against the wall, where it stuck. "Now go to fucking sleep," he said.

"I can't," she said.

He extended his legs and wiggled his toes. She did the same. They were sitting next to each other, hips touching.

"Oscar, are we getting outta hand?"

"Probably," he said.

"Well, what should we do?" she said. "Should we keep going?"

He didn't answer, but he squeezed up tight against her. When she put her arm over his shoulder and played with his nipple through his T-shirt he put his hand on her thigh through the open smock. They watched the brownie inch its way toward the floor, leaving a stain they would never completely get out.

"Oscar? Baby? Rub my butt. My butt hurts," she said.

"Goddammit, Estrella," he said. "I'm fuckin tired."

"Well, I wish you'd rub my butt and talk to me. My boobs hurt, too. But my butt especially."

He took the arrow from her skull and flung it aside and turned her over and began rubbing her butt, then he fell asleep with his forehead in the small of her back.

"Oscar?"

"What the fuck is it, Estrella? Tell me what the fuck it *is*."

"I wish you'd rub me all over," she said, turning onto her back. "My butt and boobs hurt both today." She flung open the smock exposing her breasts.

He stared at her. "You've fucking lost it, huh?"

"Oh, fuck, yes," she said, jiggling her breasts, glad the mushrooms were finally kicking in again. "When I was ten or eleven years old these were as big as they are now. You should have seen me. I grew so fast in those days my parents were ashamed. Didn't you?"

"The fuck are you talking about?"

"Didn't you ever feel your cock growing?"

"No," he said.

At last he stood, took a cigarette from his shirt pocket, lit it, and looked at the brownie. It had made it to the floor. Then he went and put his ear to the door.

She said, "I love you, Oscar. I wish you'd want to talk."

"You have chocolate on your left front tooth," he said.

She licked it off behind her lips. "Just come and lie next to me. I feel weird," she said.

He came and lay down next to her and turned to face the wall.

"Oscar?"

He farted.

"Why don't you tell me all the things you like and all the things you don't like?"

"Estrella, please," he said, "please, shut the fuck up."

"No," she said. "You shut the fuck up. I'm gonna talk."

He farted again.

"Brilliant," she said. Then: "Well...," she said, pleased with herself and the rising buzz. "I like good drugs, acid and BHO, shit like that. I like B movies and musicals, riding the Metromover, and that one time I went parasailing." She stopped. "Of course, none'a this is in order of preference. But I like that, parasailing. There's a moment as you leave the water you feel whatever happens is fine." She turned on her side and spooned him, whispering into his ear now: "I like staying up late and never going to bed. I wish we could do this all the time, not just once in a while. And I like fucking. I like to be fucked like I'm being raped. I like going to clubs and bars and drinking microbrews with friends. I like Olivia Vargas very much. I'd like to go dancing with her at least once a week. I'd like to have good drugs all the time. I'd like to be able to buy good drugs for all our friends every time they needed them without having to wait. Dino needs some mescaline for Halloween. And I'd like to get Gaby some good Colombian Pink for his big birthday bash. He's old enough. And I'd like you to get a new haircut. You really need one. You look like a hippie. I don't like hippies. And I'd like us to have a place of our own. I'd like us to have some real privacy. Most of all," she said. "Most of all I'd like us both to be able to live without any worries and just have enough money to get us high whenever we wanted and everything like that...You're asleep," she said.

"How could I possibly be asleep with you whispering all freaky in my ear like that?" he said.

"I can't think of anything else right now. Now you go. Tell me what you'd like."

"I'd like you to shut the fuck up," he said at the wall.

"Well, fuckin-A guy. I'm just talking." She took hold of the pillow.

"I just wanna —," he started to say, but she snatched the pillow from under his head and socked him on the ear with it.

"Ha!" she said. "Pow!"

"Jesus," he said, "you fucking bitch." Then: "All right, all right, let me lie here a minute, then I'll get up," he said, turning onto his back, his eyes closed. He tried to smoke, but the cigarette was broken and out. He let his hand fall to the bed.

In a while she said, "Oscar? You asleep?" She socked him again with the pillow, hard, directly down on his face, but there was no response. She sat there a while, staring at him. Then she got up and started doing jumping jacks.

She tried to not listen to her breathing, but it began to make her feel even weirder. There was a sound coming from inside her nose when she breathed. She opened her mouth and tried to regulate her breathing so that she could breathe in and out and not hear it. It was no use. The little sound in her nose made everything no use. There was a wheezy squeak in her chest too. She stopped and started doing toe touches, reaching down and touching the tip of each finger to each respective toe. She did them very fast, and she could feel the air cold against her skin beginning to break a sweat. She heard two people outside their door and she stopped with the calisthenics. Someone coughed hard and phlegmy before going away. Then she heard something plastic and expensive-sounding smash on the floor. She breathed. The toilet flushed in the bathroom, and then it flushed again. Again she breathed. She did a full Sun Salute. She held the Downward Dog part almost five minutes. She remembered something she saw in a documentary: If you get enough blood up into your brain all the oxygen'll make you feel a lot better. Or something like that. She tried a Head Stand. She held it for what seemed like a long time. She tried to relax as the blood rushed into her skull. She imagined her legs suspended by giant helium balloons and her head swathed in something gauze-like. But then she lost her balance and fell over backwards. Her heel came crashing down on the Ikea lamp on the nightstand and the nightstand fell over. She lay there on the wooden floor. The room was dark now. She thought her heel might have some plastic splinters in it. She touched her temple, where the arrow was. After a while she stood up. And then she began to feel afraid, and then in one inexplicable moment of originless terror she began to say oh fuck, oh fuck, oh fuck, oh fuck, oh fuck...

Fuck. Oh fuck.

"Oscar," she said.

There was no answer.

Then she grabbed the pillow and brought it down so hard on his face it exploded. It was magic. There were feathers everywhere, rising and falling like snow. She heard the children outside again. They seemed to have stopped in front of the apartment building next door. The children were shrieking, and the men were grumbling, and she couldn't figure out what was really going on. She didn't want to look, at least not yet. She slid her hand under her left breast and felt nothing — no beat, no warmth. She ripped off the smock and flung it aside and began to cry. She was completely naked now, and she cried and went out the door.

She washed her hands and face in the bathroom. She brushed her teeth and watched her face in the mirror. In the living room she turned off the stereo. There was no one there anymore. Then she sat down at the kitchen table. It was piled with dirty cups and dishes and lighters and ashtrays with roaches and matches in them. Hemostats and rolling papers and all other types of paraphernalia all over. A bong taller than her head. She cried again. She lit a cigarette from someone's pack on the table. After a time she walked back to the bedroom and put on one of his dress shirts that had been draped over a chair.

She looked out the front window at the shrieking children and grumbling men. It turned out to be just one child. He'd been caught in a net by the goateed men in their uniform bowler hats. They'd sheathed their billy clubs. The child was raven-haired and probably definitely rabid. He struggled against the net. And the shrieking. She couldn't bear to watch anymore. She went back to the living room and sat in the big chair. She hoped no one would come home. She paged through someone's swollen sketchbook. She gazed at the drawings and the photographs and the images and the masking tape and the writing. She heard the Dispossessed Rabid Child paddywagon pull up and a while later away. She listened until it disappeared around the bend in the road in her mind. She looked back down at the sketchbook. None of the writings made sense. The sketchbook was huge, over a hundred pages. She flipped through them all.

When it began to get dark outside she got up. The sky was flecked with little clouds just over the trees and was beginning to turn orange. The trees and the two-story apartment buildings across the street were beginning to lose shape as she watched. The sky grew oranger, then red, then redder, and then purple and the light sort of imploded rapidly behind the trees. She'd seen this thousands of times, the Earth rolling away from the sun, but she knew that none of them had been like this. Not in the movies she'd seen or in any book she'd tried to read on her iPad had an Earth rolled away so sinisterly.

She waited, and then she moved over to the door and turned the lock and stepped out onto the stoop. She let the shirt flap around her naked body. The air was hot and humid. By stages things grew darker and more invisible. She tried to let her eyes adjust to see but nothing behaved until above the sky's clouds a plane too high and far to hear left a very straight white line like a sword that hung there super still for what seemed like forever.

*

She walked through the dark apartment, back into the bedroom. He was curled fetal in the center of the bed, the covers over his torso, his head all under the open pillow. She could hardly make out what he looked like. A formless mound with doubled legs. He looked like he'd fallen from somewhere high. As she looked the room grew very dark and the white sheets made to glow and ripple grossly before her eyes.

She picked up a good pillow off the bed. He groaned. She drew the pillow way back behind her.

"The Punkrocker's Girlfriend" is a parody of Raymond Carver's story "The Student's Wife," found in the collection *Where I'm Calling From*

Not Chocolate

My kid's got this method for playing Lite Brite: We'll sit cross-legged on the living room floor, in our socks, in compliance with Mommy's no-shoes-on-the-carpet rule. Then he'll dump out all the little pegs and arrange them into groups by color until they're all around us in little piles — red, green, yellow, blue...so on. But not all the pegs of one color will be in one pile. There might be four or five piles of red, two of green, one of yellow, like that. It's totally arbitrary and serves no purpose I can see. Then he'll get up and switch the light off and draw the blinds, but the blinds leak, and if it's bright out the light leaks light up dust motes, thin lines of carpet, ridges of furniture. Finally he'll come and hand me the penlight and sit.

At first it's hard to see, just the light from the leaks and the Lite Brite light around the black paper and from behind the thing. But when my eyes adjust I can start to see more features in his face, and stray hairs lighting up blond in the glow. Eventually I can even see the tips of his fingers blanch as he works the pegs through the paper.

I always tell him it'd be more fun if we did the other way, but he always insists we do it like this.

My job, he says, is to man the penlight.

"Shine, Daddy," he says. "Here."

To find the spot where his finger points at a tiny letter.

*

There's something I think I need to tell my wife, though I'm not sure I should. I'm thinking that if I make the connection for her, which is only the truth, perhaps she'll understand, maybe sympathize, and cut me some slack. Not so that I can continue to do it. No. That's definitely not it. It's definitely not why I'd tell her. I just want her to know that it's kind of her fault, that had it not been for her, this whole thing would not be happening. It would be a non-issue.

But I don't know if I can bring myself to tell her. Not that I think she'd leave me over it or anything. I'm pretty sure of that actually, that she won't. Thing is I'm afraid of the whole scenario, what might ensue.

And the how. How to tell her is a whole other story.

*

I met Marie in college, at a bar, actually. There was no missing her: a willowy, Nordic-looking thing with silver eyes, platinum-blond hair cut short like a boy's, and one of those upturned button noses. A model type. She stood literally a head taller than everyone else. I had to look up to talk to her face.

I was a much bolder person then.

We'd only exchanged numbers that first night, but soon we took to meeting up almost nightly for drinks, which always ended at my apartment having sex. She was a knockout. Still is. Her lips blow a perpetual kiss, and she's waistless and entirely hairless, only the finest of silvery fuzz in places you'd normally expect to find real hair.

*

Last year around Easter the three of us were shopping at CVS. Fox ran up with one of those Cadbury Eggs asking could he have it. Sure, we told him. And then he asked could he eat it now. Sure, we said.

The kid took an obscenely long time eating that thing: at first just licking it, then biting the very tip off and sucking the cream out, and then licking all inside of it before eating it in tiny bites, the thin foil wrapper long ago dropped somewhere.

We were shopping for odds and ends and picking something up at the pharmacy. I had a cart and everything. But Fox still wasn't done by the time we finished shopping. He was really savoring that thing. Looking at him — all sugared-up and smiling, face a chocolate mess, eyes wild — the feeling I got was somewhere between love and disgust. We were already at the register when I went back to get Wet-Naps.

*

The thing happened about three weeks into the relationship.

We were having sex in my apartment one night when she suggested anal. But she was way more crude than that. She said: "I want you to fuck me in the ass." Unquote.

Something like this would never have even crossed my mind. Much less her asking it. Or telling it rather. I was thinking girlfriend material here.

*

It was before we got married but after we'd met that it happened. It involved a paid girl who it turned out had a friend who was friends with a friend of a friend of Marie's. They were friends way before Marie and I were friends. Lots of stuff was lost in the relating, but she'd put it together. The friend assured her there was no sex.

And there wasn't.

It was a non-issue.

*

I want you to fuck me in the ass.

It was the furthest thing from my mind.

*

She forgave me, and we moved past it, but it was the unspoken agreement that I'd never again take part in what I took part in that was the main condition under which she'd agreed to marry me.

But it's been a long time now. Seven years of unspoken agreements and a six-year-old son between us that gives me hope.

*

With the penlight I notice black outlines around the nails of his middle and index fingers, and his thumb. I ask him to let me see, but before he shows me he looks himself, first in the gesture men use, then in the one women use with the fingers out and palm down.

I tell him let me see.

"What's on your hands?" I say.

"What?" he says.

*

I didn't really want to, for several reasons. One was I'd never had anal sex, and the relationship was still kind of young for that sort of thing. And two was I was in love.

But I couldn't say no. For this there were several reasons also. So I said sure and went and found in the bathroom an old crinkled tube of KY and did it to her the way I'd imagined it was supposed to be done: in slowly, gently, easy, then out slowly. Not like porn.

It was better than I'd imagined, and everything went fine, smoothly, no mishaps. Out of politeness I'd warned her that I was coming, and she said to just come inside, and so I came inside.

Afterwards we were sitting on the edge of the bed, cuddling, kissing, holding each other. We sat like that for a while, until a minute later she excused herself to the bathroom. I was admiring her form. Her elegant hipwise walk disappeared into the bathroom when I saw through the corner of my eye something on the bed where she was sitting next to me.

*

One day we took him to Merry Christmas Park to play in the playground. We sat on a bench and watched. Fox makes fast friends wherever he goes, and there he was, standing in front of the swing set talking to the other kids there — all of them girls, four of them in swings, swinging. Only he talked, organizing some sort of game. The sun was low, came in slanted, paneled, a soft honey light.

"A little lady's man," Marie said.

"A friggin natural," I said.

The sun was at his back. His hair glowed almost white. Marie put her hand on my knee and squeezed. I looked at her. Her lips had tightened to a half-smile.

But her eyes.

I already knew.

"Baby," she said, "is there anything you need to tell me?"

*

You know how when you look at something and you think it's something else entirely even though you know exactly what it is? Well, this was like that. My initial thought was ice cream. A smallish scoop of chocolate ice cream with lines of some sort of icing or condensed milk drizzled over it. Also, the entire little thing seemed to be wrapped hermetically in cellophane. It was shiny.

*

Okay. So I relapsed. Nothing to do but confess. It was a violation of the condition. This didn't seem to be an issue, though, the first time, because she'd asked how could she help. Was there anything she could do. Like it was a problem. A problem.

Over time all of our secrets had trickled out, and we worked them, made promises and agreements, mostly unspoken.

I'll admit it did cross my mind. But there's no way. For some reason. There was no way I'd ask her to.

I didn't say anything.

*

But I knew it was a turd. It was about the size of an egg, smaller, maybe, and I was embarrassed, for her mostly because it was obvious she'd had no clue she laid a chocolate Cadbury doo doo egg on my bed.

It was almost cute, sitting there.

But I had to get rid of this thing. I got up and looked frantically around for something to grab it with. I found a sock. A plain white tube sock. I used the sock like a glove to pick the turd up off the bed. Then I inverted the sock so that the turd hung in the outside-in end of it.

My fingers smelled more like sex than shit.

*

Later I got to wondering how the hell? I'd used a different company, a different hotel, a different phone, a different city, a different everything. Then I got to wondering what kind of circles is she really in?

I pursued none of this, however.

*

Now I wasn't about to put this thing in my kitchenette's trashcan, and my apartment had only one bathroom, so I decided I'd just throw it out the window. I didn't have much time before she came out and caught me naked playing with shit in a sock. How would've I explained it: a mysterious lump dangling in the slightly brown-stained toe of a white tube sock?

Anyway. I opened the window and flung it out. I lived on the top floor of a four-story apartment building in the Gables. I flung it out as far away from the building as I could. The window overlooked the parking lot, but I didn't bother looking out or anything. I was in a hurry. And but now the bed sheet had a little brown stain on it, so I came and snatched the sheets and covers from the bed and threw them in a corner. All this took less than a minute, way less time than it takes to explain.

I sat back on the stripped bed waiting as if I hadn't done anything, and right then out she came — naked, long-curved, stunning. I was nervous until she smiled, and then everything went fine. We showered together. We ate. We even had a nightcap of warm cognac. I remember now it was winter.

*

Okay. It involves a willing call girl and a coffee table with a glass top sturdy enough to hold her weight and with space enough underneath it for me to crawl.

*

"Where've you had your hands?" I say.

"Nowhere, Daddy. What do you mean?" He holds his fingers to his nose and smells. "I don't smell anything, Daddy."

In the penlight beam it looks like chocolate. I take his wrist, bring his fingers to my nose...

Not chocolate.

I look at him in the dim light, his round face wide-open. We're done with the hat, working on the nose. I point with the penlight.

"Okay. Where?" I say.

*

I'm not too big on the Net — YouTube, Facebook, etcetera. But instead of working on this piece I spent the whole day at Starbucks with my back to a corner, surfing, listening on my headphones, watching videos, mostly, with some reading. I did not write a single word.

Most didn't seem sick. Save for the ones who touched it and played with it and ate it.

I do none of that. Nor am I interested.

So who's it hurting? Why is it "wrong"? Who makes the rules?

I turned off my laptop. I pictured Marie in school in front of a bunch of hip art students. Mrs. Marie, they call her, at New World, known as one of the cooler teachers. Kids stop her everywhere. Then I pictured Fox, at school, practicing his cursive, his little red tongue poking out the side of his mouth.

Starbucks was jam-packed with people glued to screens. I left.

Outside it was going to rain. It was more than gray. I climbed into the Jeep and put my bag in the passenger seat. It started to rain then. Big globby drops. Loud. I got out of the Jeep and slammed the door shut and stood there. In the rain.

Nothing was wrong.

*

He's improvised. Again. Little white clouds. A yellow sun. Two blue birds in the black sky. Shaped like Vs. He always uses all the pegs.

*

Later I walked her out to her car. We both saw it at the same time. The sock had hit her windshield, dead center pretty much, and had slid down and was now resting on the end of the driver's side windshield wiper. I was speechless. She said, "What *is* that?"

I shook my head.

We got up next to the car and when she reached for it I almost cried out for her to stop, to not touch it, but I couldn't rightly snitch on myself, which in turn would've meant snitching on her shitting accidentally on my bed, so I let her pick it up and inspect it.

Horrified, she quickly dropped it, at the same time stepping back from it. It lay on the blacktop between us.

Her shit in my sock.

She said, "Oh my god, dude, it's shit!" "*Shit*?" I asked. "Yes dude it's fucking shit! There's a piece of shit in there!" she said. "No fucking way!" I said. "What sick fuck would —" I said, looking around the parking lot shadows as if I'd spot the culprit.

I never told her about that.

So I guess that is one secret that never trickled out.

*

"Look, Mommy. Me and Daddy made a clown."

I didn't notice her walk in from outside. She's kneeling on the carpet next to us, still in her boots, all dirty from the garden, little clumps falling out and onto the carpet, I can see.

"It's beautiful, baby," she says. "Isn't it, honey?" She smells of wetness, of wet earth.

"It sure is," I say.

"He's a circus clown, Daddy. He's a happy clown."

We're all here, in the dark, he looking at his clown, and I looking at her look at him.

Here is something bigger than us put together.

"Marie," I say, "baby..."

Unthinkable

Was round October twenty-nine or thirty two-thousand-five that some hurricane I can't remember the name of on its way to maybe re-devastate New Orleans flanked the state and left patches of city powerless in darkness so that a curfew enforced effectively canceled all planned Halloween parties in Wynwood. But Reese, my just casual friend who allows me to sometimes frequently occupy her vaginal, anal and oral cavities, quickly noted that our particular patch of city however was still powered and lit and that she, having long labored meticulously on her costume, would have her Halloween party regardless, impulsively posting it on Facebook in spite of my and Alfredo's vehemently expressed disinterest in hosting such a party or any of its sort of people. You see I'd been holed up two weeks in the lab, subsisting solely on Blue Mountain coffee and Häagen-Daz ice cream, while Alfredo and his girlfriend Veronica stood diligently by, testing all substances produced, and we were very tired, and spent.

Reese was the only one in costume that night as Alfredo, Veronica and I stood gawking at the sheer incredibility of it. The costume. She'd told me something about being the lady from Alfred Hitchcock's classic *The Birds*, but when she emerged from the bedroom she'd spent two quiet solitary hours in, I was taken aback, at first, then impressed, then in pretty much total speechless shock for a good two minutes. She was standing there smiling. She had really pulled it off.

She had on a vintage double-breasted tweed coat and skirt and sensible pumps, and had donned a blond curled wig, her face made professionally up with little bird beak peck holes and scratches oozing fake blood all on down the coat. But the most extraordinary part of the costume was the flock of full grown birds flying around. There were two laughing gulls, three American crows, one boat-tailed grackle and two turtle doves in full-on attack poses hovering slowly around her head. She seemed to be listing slightly starboard with the weight of the gulls on that side, and I couldn't see how she would possibly negotiate doorways without turning completely sideways.

She said, "Cool, huh?"

Everyone agreed it was cool indeed.

First person to show was Yugo. He walked in carrying a big army duffle bag and was about to say something but stopped, marveling at Reese and her attack birds for a minute solid. Then he complemented her. Then we all went into Alfredo's bedroom to partake in high potency-THC G13 bong hits and the tiny pressed tablets of pure LSD-25 I synthesize in my lab oratory. (Note though that I'm positively drug free and clearheaded at all times, smoking only genetically engineered marijuana on occasion and occasionally drinking certain micro-brewed beers and artisanal batch spirits simply for their nutritional and curative values and flavors, unlike my father and brother, who have since I can remember looking up at from down in my crib — and yes my memory goes clearly back to the day I emerged from my dead whore mother's womb into the hands of my totally piss drunken father — been drunk or smashed on some household inhalant up there around my beloved colorful mobile holding bottles of cheap beer or Hi-C boxes surely spiked with some thing or other, and everyone has always told me that I am the clearest head in the family as well as amongst my friends).

Rifling through Yugo's big army duffle bag, trying to figure which costume would suit me, I all of a suddenly realized Alfredo had already transformed quite seamlessly into a very convincing Lone Ranger complete with swirl-stitched leather cowboy boots with spurs that jangled, a curlicued western shirt plus red neckerchief, and a double hip holster for the silver plastic filigreed revolvers he then aimed at me.

"Pow, pow," he said under the black leather face mask.

Veronica too had metamorphosed unseen into a small-human-size version of a sluttish Tinkerbell. She held a thin LED-tipped magic wand that sparkly trailed between her thumb and forefinger. It also made a tiny tinkling sound I was quite sure only I could hear. Her wings bounced in the smoke and the light from Alfredo's various Feng Shuily placed Ikea lamps and flat screen Apple monitors.

Soon Yugo was barefoot and naked climbing into a neon green slingshot swimsuit. It cradled perfectly his package slung tightly over each dark nipple's skin whose curly little black hairs clawed at the stretchy fabric there. Then he put on the most lurid Mardi Gras mask ever. Its gaudy bird of paradise feathers rivaled in size to Reese's flock of angry birds. Out the eye holes his eyes peered up and down and side to side all primitive-like, reminding me of something from some dark wet jungle. Yugo is dark and tall and kind of fat with a greasy complexion.

Everyone agreed he in his costume looked like nothing any of us had ever seen or could name.

At this point it was on me. I could feel the room's vibrations: *Choose a costume already*, it said, unsaid. And since I had already attempted the guises of several classic monster hybrids —Frankula, Drancenstein, Mummywolf, etcetera — and deemed them all unsuitable for the warmth with which they provided my face, I was standing there mid-dress in low top Chucks with black socks pulled half way up my knees, white with black pinstripe boxers and an old wife beater. I saw this image in the full-length mirror on the back of Alfredo's bedroom door and figured, what with my hair grown wild and uncombed and beard gone woolly, that I looked exactly like the slob I had become the two weeks in the lab, and so to finish it off I took from Yugo's bag a sleazy like silk robe with wide red and gray vertical stripes, and donned it, saying to my friends,

"I'm a slob."

Everyone agreed it was good.

We had been in that room for some time now, and I had lost track of time, and it had grown hard to see for all the smoke and they were listening to some kind of music I could not hear, and it was due to this aural malfunction that I was able to at that moment in Alfredo's thick smoke-filled room hear voices on the other side of Alfredo's bedroom door. And the voices were many.

Opening the door I was shocked to find the apartment jam-packed with life forms, characters from comic strips, movies, fairy tales, TV shows and every walk of human and in some cases even nonhuman life. I walked slowly into the throng, not trying to recognize any one but simply tallying the life forms there.

There were three Imperial Storm Troopers, two Darth Vaders, one Darth Maul and one Chewbacca, all of them shaking hands introducing themselves in a tight circle, weapons at ease. Animal, Kermit the Frog, Big Bird and Oscar the Grouch in his can were there, none of them together. Ex-presidents Richard Nixon and Ronald Reagan conversed in the foyer, while a gory-headed John F. Kennedy danced with Marilyn Monroe in a gorilla suit and a bikini-clad girl with a gorilla mask on. There was a fat ninja and a skinny ninja, and there were Ninja Turtles, only three of them. Bruce Banner was there but not as the Hulk only green still at the dining room table rolling cigarettes, clothes shredded and tattered. In the kitchen were a giant taco, a giant hot dog, two police men, one prostitute, three firemen, one National Indian or Native American in generic headdress, a ballerina and Freddy Krueger, all of them partaking in the plethora of myriad hallucinogens stored in my refrigerator. Jason and Zorro struck machete against sword over and around the coffee table where the Party Avenger spoke animatedly with his like eighty-year-old self, who leaned on a walker and had his wiffle ball bat tucked under one arm. I wondered who the old man could be until I realized it was not but a really good full-body makeup job. Celia Cruz and Johnny Walker played tonk on one side of the kitchen-slash-dining room bar, while along the adjoining bar Van Gogh and a white Bob Marley picked flowers from the plants there for a bowl. Reese was now interfacing with Alfred Hitchcock himself, and on the living room's dance floor the Toxic Avenger attempted to break dance, the lengths of his limbs' toes and fingers slinging everywhere slapping Wonder Woman and Superman.

My headcount was now up to past forty, surely, and that was just inside.

I began to wonder about our safety and the safety of our downstairs neighbors directly beneath the wooden floor I felt slightly shaking under my feet with the weight of the life forms mingling and dancing, until I actually spotted our downstairs neighbors with us in the throng as Tarzan, Jane, Boy and Cheetah. They even had a real live chimpanzee on a leash. It kept looking back and frantically forth between the Marilyn Monroe and bikini-clad gorillas.

Soon I ventured outside where someone handed me a cold Erdinger's saying "Great party, man. Cheers," and attempted a toast and handshake simultaneously, managing only to spill some of the Erdinger's down the front of my wife beater from the neck on down in a big brown V out on the front porch balcony, where all of a suddenly I realized all the strange and out of place and odd and sort of like reject costumes had gathered. Here, there, there and there. There was a guy with party hats on his ears and a just-average-size dildo strapped to his nose and mouth, so that they were cock and balls respectively. He could not really talk or drink his beer or smoke his cigarette without first pushing the cock up to lift the balls up off his mouth. Another guy seemed to have attempted a bona fide mummy but had run out of gauze way early on. A girl in just a bra with a wig stuffed in it and eyeliner mustache and beard claimed she was the bearded hairy-chested lady. I cannot accurately describe the others out there, but suffice it to say there were several with wigs and unskillfully applied makeup and sunglasses.

The girl who then appeared coming up the crowded stairs to the apartment with an un-costumed companion in tow wore a bright yellow leotard and sandals, and every exposed skin and hair and nail dyed or painted the same bright yellow color. Even her eyes shone yellow. When I asked her what she was she said she was the sun, at which point I noticed in her mouth her teeth and tongue too were yellow, and her voice registered in my head as Una's.

"Wow," I said.

"This is my new boyfriend, Dustin," she said indicating the suit and tie standing beside her with two plastic Publix bags of Peter Pan peanut butter, creamy. They went inside and through the window I saw Una open up one by one the jars on the counter near where the giant hot dog and the giant taco argued, gesticulating with thumbless lettuce hands and relish arms, while Dustin fashioned from a big red keg beer cup and rubber band a sort of snout. Then Una the Sun began to slather peanut butter all on Dustin's face and hair, working it in with her fingers, and then a comb, until she'd sculpted the ears and hairdo and ridged snout — using Tic-Tacs for teeth and knuckle holes for nostrils — of the head of the star of the late eighties TV sitcom ALF. It was splendid: the formally dressed Peanut Butter ALF.

Everyone outside and inside agreed with its greatness.

The commotion of this drew everyone's attention, including Alfredo the Lone Ranger, who approached Peanut Butter ALF and said,"I am ALF."

"I too am ALF," said Peanut Butter ALF.

I listened clearly to this exchange through the window, and it was then that my attention moved to the sidewalk below's clopping of hooves and neighing of horse, to see the by far most extraordinary sight of the night thus far: a glittery pink unicorn making its way toward the building and then up the crowded stairs to enter the apartment. I followed. It began to dance around on the all of a suddenly cleared living room's dance floor. Everyone cheered. Then here came ALF the Lone Ranger hi-hoing with his lasso trying to make it Silver, but he could not, as it bucked and bucked and broke in two exposing Maite's unmistakable ass out the hole of the unicorn's front legs and neck and head part, and then up stood Tony, sweating, spectacles fogged, out of the unicorn's ass end.

That's when I heard the phone ring. I went and answered it. I was standing next to Darth Maul and Van Gogh each filliping his own little baggie of cocaine hydrochloride. On the phone: my brother's voice.

"The sun shines even at night, bro, take note."

I slammed the phone down. I stared lost in thought for a minute.

When I turned I faced Reese under her birds all askew and she squirted my V-shaped dark beer stain with fake blood out of a little tube and said, "The police are here. They wanna talk to you."

"Me?" I said.

"You're the only one of us that can talk to them, you know that."

She did have a point there so I went down as is — a slob in a dark V-shaped-beer-stained bloody wife beater and a sleazy robe with said beer in hand to talk to the two cops, who had their MIAMI-DADE POLICE cop cars double-parked on the street.

Cop One said, "Is that your party up there?"

"Yes, sir, so it seems," I answered.

Then Cop Two said, "Well, we need you to shut it down. We've had complaints from the neighbors."

"Shut it down, sir? What exactly do you mean by that?" I asked, "Shut it down?"

"I mean shut it down," Cop Two repeated.

"So you're saying," I said, "and correct me if I'm wrong, sir, that you want me to send fifty plus people up there drunk into the street?"

Cop One and Cop Two exchanged a look. "Hold on," one of them said and they stepped away and conversed.

I looked back up over my shoulder at the apartment and saw every conceivable shape of face staring weirdly out the windows and from the front porch balcony. The vibe was eerie, to say the least. Then I turned back my attention to the cops.

"Okay, look," Cop One said, "from here on the rest of this cul-de-sac is your property, basically, so this is what you're gonna do: You're gonna clear the apartment — "

"Probably a fire hazard that many people up there anyway," Cop Two interrupted.

" — turn off the music," Cop One continued, "stop serving drinks, then usher them all onto the street and sidewalk here where they're gonna sober up. I want the street clear by three a.m."

"We're gonna cordon off the street for you," Cop Two added.

"Do you copy?" Cop One pressed.

"Copy, sir. Ten four, loud and clear," I said.

Soon the cops cordoned the street off with bright orange and white reflective barricades produced from the trunks of their MIAMI-DADE POLICE cop cars, and then they planted flares that melted into the asphalt. I employed Yugo and Alfredo the Lone Ranger to help usher everyone out into the street. Yugo went around in his slingshot swimsuit and Mardi Gras mask imposingly waving his arms around shouting "Out! Out! Everybody out!" while ALF the Lone Ranger did the same, sort of, silently shepherding everyone at plastic gunpoint.

The apartment was almost empty when I saw the pirate. He had a real peg leg and an eye patch and a hook and a live parrot on one shoulder, bad breath and teeth and a stink involved as if gone unbathed for months.

I told him he had to leave. He responded accordingly, the way I had totally expected of a pirate. A real pirate.

Then the phone rang. I answered it. It was many voices layered, almost singing in a steady crescendo, my brother's voice included.

"*Gold fish birds in lines in trees outside. Remember!*"

I slammed the phone down.

Then I went to the window and watched serenely the goings on downstairs, the apartment behind me all of a suddenly empty and quiet, until Piano Concerto Number Twenty in D Minor, Second Movement steadily rose. I lost track of time, lost in the slow unfolding of battles in the street below between the Imperial Storm Troopers, Darth Vader, Darth Maul and Chewbacca and Freddy Krueger, Jason, Zorro and the two Party Avengers while the Toxic Avenger now break danced for real on some cardboard, while Oscar the Grouch fit perfectly in with the row of trash cans along the wooden fence where a small crowd of ex-presidents, gorilla girls, superheroes and the ballerina gathered and mingled. By now the giant hot dog and the giant taco were really fighting, exchanging padded blows with edible arms. The two police men and three firemen plus prostitute and Celia Cruz hung now out with the real cops where their MIAMI-DADE POLICE cop cars were still double-parked. Tarzan, Jane, Boy and their monkey invited Animal and Kermit the Frog into their apartment downstairs. The fat ninja and the skinny ninja leaned into a chain link fence across the street making deeply out in the dark as the Ninja Turtles followed the dildo faced boy to his car where the bearded hairy-chested lady waited. Reese stood talking intimately now with Alfred Hitchcock, who, out on the front lawn, held up one of her laughing gulls while the pirate's parrot courted Reese's remaining birds unsuccessfully. Una the Sun used our downstairs neighbor's hose to hose Peanut Butter ALF's head off. It took a lot of time and lots of water but what a splendid transformation it was!

Everyone agreed.

I could tell.

Then the phone rang. It had been ringing a long time, actually. I went and turned the stereo off and answered it. It was my father's voice singing me Happy Birthday. He sang the song the whole way through.

"Thanks, Dad," I said.

"Happy Birthday, son," he said.

I listened to him ring off. I placed the phone back gently in its cradle. I looked at the sundial on the wall. It was two thirty-four AM, not my birthday. I glanced at the scene downstairs through the window, then back at the eight-point buck crashing through the wall, then quickly at the small baby bamboo stand growing out of the bear fish bowl table and all of a suddenly an old crossbow was in my hand. I couldn't remember how it got there when I began to think the unthinkable.

"Unthinkable" was inspired by David Foster Wallace's short story "John Billy," found in the collection *Girl With Curious Hair*.

Missing

Night. The Atlantic Ocean.

You can see in silver light seven dorsal fins huddled together abob in the black water. In the water's divots dance sequins of reflected stars and the occasional filigree of one shooting across the sky. There is no moon, only stars, and the stars' points are sharp. They hang up there without twinkling and, down here, a negative sort of wind sucks air for complete stillness. The air is clear, and the only sounds are the purl of seawater on the dolphins' backs and the plosive *push* and breathy *who* from their nostrils, their blowholes.

What you hear is the cetacean equivalent of a snore.

*

Victor Llanez and Brian Knopf launch Victor's boat into the water at one of the ramps at Black Point Marina. It's late. No one else is at the docks. All night Brian's been talking nonstop about dreams, trying to get to a point; Victor knows and has tuned his listening to selective, offering Yeahs, Wows, No Ways and Say Agains at just the right moments, waiting for an opening.

While Victor goes and parks his Jeep in the lot, Brain waits in the boat. Brian likes nights with stars and no moon. He goes into the cooler's ice for a Delirium Tremens, uncorks it and drinks. Then he goes back into the cooler and comes out with a can of Pabst Blue Ribbon, opens it and places it in the console's cup holder for Victor. Standing there he sighs and takes another swig, looking up at the stars.

Soon Victor returns. He hops in, starts up the Yamaha, reverses the boat and drinks his beer. All this he does fast and at the same time. Brian is standing there looking confused at his beer, until they're going forward and Victor relaxes, settling into the captain's chair. They're idling out through the channel when Brian finally sits. He starts talking:

"So it wasn't a dream per se, you know. Like I was half-asleep and half-awake. As if the dream were somehow incomplete."

Victor finds his opening. "You mean like a dolphin."

"Whadaya mean 'you mean like a dolphin?'"

"I mean the way a dolphin sleeps. It sleeps one side of its brain at a time. Does this thing called logging where it half-floats and half-swims at the surface, keeping its blowhole exposed and say its left eye closed while its right brain sleeps, and dreams."

"No shit, for real?"

"Yes shit, for real. Then at some point in the night it'll switch eyes and sleep its brain's other hemisphere. It's called unilateral sleep."

"I didn't know that. So anyway this girl in the dream was—"

"They sleep in pairs or in pods, keeping their awake eyes on the pod's periphery. Then they'll all switch positions, like reconfigure the pod when they switch eyes and brains."

"That's interesting...So this girl right, she was—"

"Like that they can watch for predators and still get some shuteye for a full-night's host of dolphin dreams."

There's a pause.

"Uh, Victor, what the fuck would a dolphin dream about?"

"Wouldn't say I know for sure. But I'm guessing pretty solidly that the dreams dreamily take place underwater, and involve the aural aspects of echolocation, and probably definitely other fellow dolphins, and maybe scholarly explosions of baitfish or something."

"I didn't know dolphins had eyelids."

"Eyelids they have."

"...."

"So you were saying about this dreamgir—"

"Never mind," Brian says, seeing they've passed the NO WAKE zone. He knows that from now on talking would be pointless. Victor pushes the Yamaha to full throttle. The engine wails them into the night.

*

A Doppler-effected whine. Sounds like a tiny chainsaw loudening toward the pod. Their single eyes open all at once and, using a primordial sort of GPS, the pod turns north, with the Gulf Stream. One of them issues a squeak then two clicks; the rest echo in linear sync. A sort of roll call. They sound like *push* and *who* and disappear northward like things that never were as the tiny chainsaw grows huge.

Tear-assing through is Victor and Brian in *The Bone Machine*, heading due east at about twenty knots. On board the throttled-up Yamaha wails, peals, whines, roars louder than hell, and what Victor and Brian see is all starlit blackness, a ghostly silver cast across a barely rippled night ocean. Behind them Miami's glow recedes. In the Yamaha's wake a roiling soup of noctiluca blooms electric-cyan whorls of sea foam. The Panga coasts as if on a road, or something even smoother, its wind in their half-smiling faces.

Victor sits starboard in the seat behind the console, his left hand on the wheel's chrome and his right wrapped around the wet cold PBR can in his Levis crotch. To Victor the sky looks like an enormous Lite Brite set in which some giant kid punctured a bunch of random holes but left no pegs. Victor is at the peak of his life, in more ways than one, and, next to him, on the port side's cushion, Brian tips his DT bottle's ass at the stars, his NRA cap, which he wears like a tongue in his apolitical cheek, turned rakishly backwards to not lose it in the boat wind.

Brian and Victor are best friends. They're out here tonight to square with the planet. With them in *The Bone Machine* they have an Igloo full of Pabst Blue Ribbon and Delirium Tremens, and bungee-corded to the rings on the Panga's deck is an ammo case, black, twice the size of the Igloo, containing bundles of giant bottle rockets and roman candles, knots of old rags, five or six big bottles of CVS-brand isopropyl alcohol, a shitload of boxes of 20-gauge flares, 12-gauge SS #6 birdshot, and .223 tracers (blue); plus a 20-gauge brass flare gun, a 12-gauge Citori double barrel, and an AR-15. For Brian and Victor this is a six-year-old, twice annual birthday ritual: coming out here in the middle of the night in the middle of the dark to get tanked on their birthdays and launch all types of fiery shit at the universe: flares at roman candles for cosmic collisions, isopropyl Molotov cocktails tossed then shot with the shotgun only to watch them explode, tracers at bottle rockets for sometimes direct hits, and other extemporized pyromaniacal experiments. Victor calls it

Getting Right With The Planet. Brian says it's Absolutely Fucking Beautiful Man. Brian's birthday is April 1st. Victor's is September 17th. Today is Victor's birthday, he's twenty-seven, and he has a headful of only-god-knows-how-much acid.

Victor, a self-proclaimed Strictly Hallucinogens Man (though he does occasionally drink), throttles down and cuts the engine and running lights. Their wake fizzles to silence, and compared to the Yamaha's wailing a second ago this silence is loud. *The Bone Machine* scuds along as Victor looks around: starry, quiet, the absolute zero wind, uncommon out here, sort of spooks him. "So whadaya think? Here good?"

"Victor-Man, it's your birthday." Brian, a vegetarian who also considers himself straightedge since Alcohol Is Food, Not A Drug, downs his DT and onto the deck with Victor's spent PBR can the bottle rolls.

"Okay then." Victor takes from his hip pocket a blue Bic lighter and a Pyrex pipe shaped like a cock with balls, the balls part being the bowl, and packs it with a dime-size nugget of medicinal pot he takes from a Ziploc that was also in the pocket. Victor then smokes from the pipe's cock's head.

Brian gets up and goes to the Igloo's ice for another DT and uncorks it and takes a nice, long, pull, standing before Victor smoking in the captain's chair. Brian's pretty tanked. He sways like the ocean but the ocean is still. Brian's always taken aback by the Atlantic's 360° blackness, its desolateness. He swivels his head from shoulder to shoulder, slowly, considering the space of sea, the googol of stars above and below, the how fucking far from everywhere they are. Brian's cap is still turned needlessly backwards. "Victor-Man." Brian says *Victor-Man* only when he's good and drunk. "Victor-Man. You gonna tell me that you're such a good nautical navigator, technical sea wonk, thalassic expert like your expert CIA sea frogman dad taught you, such a good old Magellan Old Ahab dude of these chemically, troubled, times boy that if I take this here boat of yours in any outward directional direction for however long I please you can astronomically, deadly reckon your way back to Black Point using neither GPS nor compass but just that god, damned, mess, of holy stars up there?"

By no means is Victor tanked — he's had maybe three PBRs, tops — but he is tripping balls and now stoned too, which is another thing altogether. But Victor is an inveterate acid eater who feels LSD and THC, his only two real drugs of choice, especially in combination, heighten his ken, as if normally primordially unused parts of his brain were activated by the combination. In fact, Victor had taken most of his important college exams at the U of M on LSD plus THC and had thus graduated with a flying and colorful 3.8 GPA tacked to a biochemical degree in biochemistry, and to celebrate that Victor had taken upwards of fifteen hits of near-Sandoz-grade LSD-25 on his graduation day, and those in the know know and can see clearly his acid's peak in the picture that sits on his dad's living room's coffee table: Victor Llanez in cap and gown, his handsome face recalling old Spanish blood, flexing strangely, brown irises overwhelmed to mere outlines by cavernous pupils, and the smile he wears says he either loves to death the person taking the picture or has taken way too much of something crazy at some point or other and has maybe never recovered. Victor hits the Pyrex cock in his mouth, holds it, and speaks to Brian in the holding-a-hit voice heard in college dormrooms the world over: "Brain-Man, you putting me to the test?"

Brian tips the DT bottle's ass heavenward, letting a small beer fall gush down his gullet. Brian's Adam's apple moves not when he drinks. He removes the bottle from lips like a failed kiss and sighs and says: "Yes. This, is only, a test."

Victor gets up from the captain's chair and steps aside, and with his lighter hand gestures at something invisible in the air to his right. "Captain Brain, be my guest," he says, sitting on the port side cushion Brian rode on their way out here, where he proceeds to cash the bud in his bowl's balls.

Brian sits in the captain's chair.

"Okay so how the fuck do you do this?"

"Push the key in and turn it to the right." Victor empties the cashed bowl by covering with his pipe hand's thumb the ball's carb and then blowing into the cock. "Now that stick-shift-thing there, that's the throttle. Depress the red button underneath its lip and push it forward, slowly, to make the boat go forward." Victor replaces Bic and Pyrex

cock-n-balls pipe in his hip pocket and sits there in the boat wind. He
runs his fingers over his shorn head. He can feel tiny wind rivers
coursing through, the hairs, up there, as Brian gets *The Bone Machine*
moving forward, steadily increasing its knottage, his DT held in his
cargo shorts crotch.

Soon Victor gets up for another PBR from the cooler and sits
back down and then opens the *ksh*. He drinks. Brian ups the Yamaha to
full throttle. Twenty knots feels a lot faster over water. Like flying. Victor
looks up at the Big Dipper's pointers, finds Polaris at the Little Dipper's
handle, which he can't actually see from here, then at Orion's Belt and at
the one visible Cassiopeia leg that without looking over at the console's
compass tells him Brian's direction is generally Andros Islandward.

In about a minute Brian is overwhelmed by the rush of
momentum and hollers "WOOOO!" Victor looks to his right, smiles at
the Brain-Man's pointy streamlined face screaming then tipping his DT
bottle's ass up with his dirty blond locks juddering underneath the bill of
his backward cap and his stupid little golden hoop earring
"YEEEAAAH!" man, and Victor silently laughs, almost out of his
control, the deep-down acid laugh. He drinks, and Brian:
"WOOOOYEEEAAAH!"

The Yamaha wails. Phosphorescent algea cyanadizes *The Bone
Machine*'s wake and, in the northwest sky above and behind them, a
meteor shower rends the atmosphere, exposing brief white slits of
cosmic meat.

Brian tear-asses like never before in his life, and screams. Victor
stands and turns and climbs up onto the Panga's poling platform above
the Yamaha. He sits down and wraps his legs and feet around the
platform's poles. Then he grips the platform between his thighs with his
left hand like a cow rider and drinks with his right, flying over the ocean,
the wind in his face smiling with teeth. Brian's DT's ass is mostly up and,
behind them, still, black heaven and sea burst blue, white, green and
from all the planet's light shows they flee.

*

Brian Knopf works an intern's position at the Miami-Dade County Morgue. Brian takes pictures of dead bodies. Brian's job is deeply intriguing and has completely changed his view on death. The moribund are no longer sad mysteries and Brian's developed a weird sort of necrophilia. During the last year or so Brian's been working at the morgue he's begun this thing with relating grimly detailed and breathless descriptions of what happens to your body after you die, like how if they don't know exactly what your cause of death was and your body requires an autopsy the coroners will make that telltale Y-shaped incision in your chest and sickeningly crack your chest cavity open and pull all your guts and organs out and systematically place all your guts and organs on a stainless steel gurney right next to you and poke at your guts and organs with really dire-looking stainless steel instruments and rods that look like car antennae or those pointers professors use until they figure out what killed you and then when they're done the coroners will take all your guts and organs and stuff them into a heavy-duty clear like garbage bag and zip tie it shut and put it into your vivisected torso and just close you up so that when you're lying in a casket all dressed up with your family hovering around the room your insides are not at all what they used to be but more like a big hot and sour soup in a bag inside your now pretty much empty torso, talk about violated, or how they have to glue your eyelids shut with Krazy Glue so you don't look emptily up at your family from inside your casket, or how the coroners sometimes swordfight with severed limbs, or how they have to wire your jaw shut so you don't give everyone in your family the howling goospers with your suddenly rictusized dead face, or how Brian's job entails a janitorial aspect he'd rather not talk about, but then talks about, adding really unnecessary and gruesome details, and maybe the weirdest thing about Brian's morgue job is the whole alone-but-un-alone factor, how he usually works late at night when most of the rest of Miami is horizontal and he's in there, alone but surrounded by a different type of horizontal people so that he's never truly really alone, which works a whole new angle on the word *alone*, and how the security cameras trained on his work stations imbue the whole alone-but-un-alone dilemma with 101 new flavors since the spooks who are always watching him are watching him but watching him after the fact, meaning they're not watching him now but later, watching him when he's alone, but not alone.

The Miami-Dade County Morgue provides Brian with all the digital photo equipment and special downward-facing quadripods required to take the postmortem pre- and post-autopsy mug shots of the dead, but lately Brian's been bringing his own personal digital memory card to covertly slip in and out of the camera so he can steal pictures of the more memorably dead, like the guy who blew his brains out but somehow remained with a grotesque smile frozen to his face and his exit-wound temple like gone, or the morbidly obese woman who looks less human than like Jabba The Hut, or that charred- and crispy-looking thing that doesn't look even remotely like a person but is, in fact, a person. The pilfered postmortem mug shots Brian's been collecting and keeping in his computer in his apartment on Biscayne have been inspiring his art and music in ways he's never dreamed. He paints portraits from the pictures and writes songs about guts and organs and nerdy severed-limb-swordfighting coroners and being alone / un-alone, and watched.

Brian Knopf is the mastermind behind the local postpunk art rock band nonpareil The Amazing Hair Drug, whose live performances not only involve music but also pornographic sock puppet shows, perverse bedizenment and über crowd involvement during which fans are sometimes hurt both physically *and* psychologically. Brian had started the band soon after graduating high school with colors with Victor Llanez on drums and socks and fire and Sabrina Muñoz on bass and socks and bikini and Alex Trujillo on lead guitar and keys and sock sounds and food- and sometimes vomit-launch. The Amazing Hair Drug has an East Coast Tour planned to begin at Churchill's (Brian says Don't miss it) on Thanksgiving Eve.

But anyway.

Brian's been wanting to confess to Victor something that happened the other day at work at the morgue but is afraid Victor will tell him exactly what he doesn't want to hear and thus reinforce Brian's thoughts on what he thinks is just plain well Brian doesn't even want to go there. Here's what happened: They brought into the morgue the body of a twenty-one-year-old girl named Sukey Nailer who'd died supposedly in a car wreck. The first thing Brian noticed about the new dead body was the very pretty toe — whose toenail was painted hot pink, by the way — on which the toe tag with Sukey Nailer's un-vital stats hung. When Brian uncovered the body he just stood there for a minute, slack-jawed, silent, before an obscenely gorgeous dead body with chocolate-colored hair and olive skin, entirely hairless, lithe, heavenly fucking beautiful and all peaceful-looking with her eyes closed as if sleeping, not a thing wrong with her save for a tiny bruise half-hidden by her hairline. Brian was alone with her, alone but not alone and being watched but after the fact. Brian's been wanting to tell someone, namely Victor, about how as he worked taking Sukey's picture he grew nervous, like the kind of nervous he gets when about to approach a girl like at a bar or a club or something, about how he sweated in the cold morgue and experienced the crotch-warmth that comes right before a hard-on and then finally how he actually got a hard-on staring at her right-there honeydew-shaped tits, her waistless hips, her shaved *oh jesus*, how vaguely in his head Brian had machinated figuring out where exactly in the morgue he could be with her out of security camera line of sight, how he sweated and crazily shook taking Sukey Nailer's picture, and how finally Brian put his back to the cameras and took his right hand's latex glove off and gently placed the ungloved hand on Sukey's flat tummy and felt the cold, dead, skin.

Brian has Sukey's picture at home in his Mac. Brian wants to tell all this to his best friend Victor, who hasn't any sort of real legitimate job other than peddling pot and acid to friends and friends' friends and friends' friends' friends so that from the profit Victor can smoke pot and drop acid for free and live fin-to-gill so to speak and pay for gas so he can go out on *The Bone Machine* and pelagic hunt for dolphin and tuna and grouper and hogfish and snatch Florida bugs up from under rocks and coral heads, and so Victor lives basically off seafood he hunts himself and THC and LSD and seawater and is kind of missing an entire wrench up there, meaning Brian's afraid Victor will act as Brian's own conscience-overriding, shoulder-mounted devil and say . . .

Victor, up on *The Bone Machine*'s poling platform, flying warp speed over the Atlantic's nighttime doldrums, finishes his PBR and throws it down at the deck in front of him next to Brian, who keeps going "WOOOO!" and "YEEEAAAH!" over the Yamaha's wailing. Then, making to adjust his legs' grip on the platform's poles, he unwraps his shins and the fronts of his Chucks, gripping now only with his hands on either side of the platform he sits on. But right at this moment the boat grinds into a patch of choppy water. Brian goes "WOOOO!" Victor's ass goes bumpily backward until his hands lose their grips and under his ass the platform is no more. He watches his Chucks carom off the stars and over his head. Brian goes "YEEEAAAH!" and Victor back flops into the Yamaha's phosphorescently foamy wake.

Jumping into the ocean is like an everyday thing for Victor. He does it pretty much every time he goes out on *The Machine*. But we have to remember now that Victor is tripping balls and stoned too and also a little drunk, and so his first thought is this a-rational this-is-my-rent-money concern to save the five sheets of acid in his wallet, which are inside his jeans' ass pocket. He is immediately treading water, holding the wallet high above his head. The stars and noctiluca frothing all around him afford a faint bluish-whitish light. He holds the leather wallet with his left hand while he inspects its contents with his right. This operation's backdrop is the Milky Way. He sees three of the 2-1/2" squares of unperforated blotter are wet. This is the highest-quality-on-the-planet LSD-25 stuff Victor refers to simply as *Beautiful*, not to by any means be wasted, and so Victor lets the three wetly ruined sheets drop to the water, which is beginning to calm and quiet its hiss and de-phosphoresce, and takes the other two unwet sheets and folds them and sticks them into his mouth. All this happens in seconds, it just takes a minute to explain. Because Victor is perhaps thinking that Brian will quickly notice Victor's sudden absence and turn around or stop or at least slow down, or perhaps Victor has absently forgotten how far out he is and thinks he can easily swim back to shore, or perhaps Victor is just not thinking, treading water, chewing on two sheets of good acid, watching the Panga's stern light recede Africaward. And now, with the wallet still high above his head, he not-so-quickly realizes his situation and spits the soggy papers out of his mouth — which is sort of pointless, he knows, because the human tongue acts like a sponge that almost instantly absorbs every last microgram of LSD, in this case about 60,000, micrograms, which is, to say the least, quite a bit — and says: "Fuck."

Victor shoves the wallet into his underwater hip pocket. He thinks he can hear Brian tinily going "woooo!" as the Panga's running light becomes the ocean's ripples' sequins. Victor kicks his Chucks off and imagines them sinking for hours, losing a quarter of a shoe size for every atmosphere of pressure until they're just a pair of baby-size Chuck Taylors down there in the dark. He sees Miami's glow in the west, which from here looks dim and dingy. Victor is calm, though. He can do this. SOP in a situation like this is to breathe slowly and deeply, swim on his back to conserve energy, meaning half-float and half-swim, and just get home. And so Victor heads homeward, westward on his back, watching the stars go insane. It's quiet out here now, obscenely beautiful. Victor sort of meditates on that.

Meantime, Brian, still tear-assing someplace toward the Eastern Hemisphere, senses vaguely a negative presence behind him and looks over his left shoulder to see no Victor. Brian's initial fright is absurd, cold, and he almost vomits. His drunk vanishes. It takes Brian a few seconds to figure frantically out how to throttle down. Finally he cuts the engine and begins to holler Victor's name into the starry watery blackness, where his cries for Victor seem only to echo.

Victor is too far in to hear his name. His ears are underwater anyway, listening to the sea's hush, watching the stars fall, trying to keep his equipoise for the soon fall out of himself.

Brian's nonstop uncontrollable with "VICTOR!" and "Holy fuck!" and "Holy shit VICTOR!" and "What the fuck my jesus fuck VICTOR!" and so on.

Victor's stars begin to oscillate. He's in that liminal zone between tripping balls and *really* tripping balls. The sky looks like a giant black sheet with millions of pinholes in it in front of the sun while the sheet tucks and pops like a sail. The ocean hushes and squeaks in his ears. He logs westward, inward.

Brian calms himself and breathes. "Okay. Okay." He takes the mini Mag-Lite Velcroed to the console and twists it on and scampers to the Panga's bow and opens the drywell and scrabbles around inside for the Q beam. Everything Brian does on this boat takes him a long and clumsy time. After several un-illuminating attempts he gets the Q beam plugged into the right outlet in the console and begins to scan both steadily and shakily the ocean for Victor. The water is so flat the Q beam's beam reflects off it and up into the sky for a great distance. Brian pans 360° around the boat several times. Brian is for once truly alone, out here. This frightens him to his existential core. He cries out Victor's name. It echoes. Then it's quiet again. Only the lap of sea on hull. He scans empty water for several minutes, hoping like he's never hoped before, his stomach turning in on itself like a Klein bottle. It feels like hours before it occurs to him:

"Flares!"

He sets the Q beam down and takes the Mag-Lite from his cargo shorts pocket and twists it on and puts it in his mouth to hold between his teeth. Then he goes and unlatches the ammo case. Brian's hands shake as he loads a flare into the gun and fires it at the sky, calling out Victor's name over the flare's pop and hiss.

Victor sees in the east-southeast sky the flare's spiraled arc, orange and beautiful, and stares, treading water now, for several minutes until the orange dust settles on the ocean, fizzles, and it's night again, and the stars. Victor has on no socks, has somehow lost them between there and here, but fails to notice. He sees in the distance the Q beam's blunt white finger pointing jaggedly everywhere over the water and into the sky. He guesstimates that Brian and *The Bone Machine* are like way too many east-southeast clicks away to be even worth trying to swim to. It would mean swimming against the current, and in the opposite direction of home. Victor thinks he's better off swimming home himself. I can do nine miles easy. Plus who knows which way Brian'll go when he starts to go. And so Victor is back on his back, breathing, half-swimming half-floating, listening to the hush and squeak of the ocean, watching the stars go insaner.

Brian doesn't know how to work a GPS. He doesn't know how to use a compass. Brian doesn't know shit from shit out here, he admits. The Q beam is off. He twists the Mag-Lite off and looks around at the blackness reflecting the universe. Totally alone. It's actually not that dark, but he can't see Victor.

"This is fucking crazy."

Brian sees Miami's glow in the west. Or what he believes is west. That *has* to be Miami, he hopes. Brian's actually doing a pretty good job at not all-out apeshitly panicking. He starts the Yamaha. He turns the wheel and heads toward the glow, just idling, slowly, not too loudly, panning the water with the Q beam, another flare at the ready.

Victor watches the Big Dipper spin counterclockwise in a parallactic arc across the sky but somehow never leaving the sky and what comes out its ladle looks like milk with BBs in it. The milky BBs cover the whole sky and hang there, threatening to fall and when they fall they fall one at a time making not the sound of one BB hitting water but the sound of millions, having little seizures before they come loose from the milk and fall, one at a time, with crazy unexpected sounds, they fall. This falling of milky BBs seems to take forever and no matter how many BBs fall their numbers are never decreased as Victor's left brain begins slowly to seep out his right ear into the Gulf Stream swirling north toward the Carolinas. He makes no attempt to keep his brain inside his head. Things here constantly change. The lacteal BBs fall from the sky like coins, like rain, like Lite Brite pegs that float showering into the water all around, like rain and there's thunder and lightning and the ocean in his ears hums and hushes, clicks and squeaks and thumps its heart. The sea underneath and all around him glows green. It murmurs on his skin, in his ears, around his face and courses its way in both real and imagined rivulets through his head's hair. He feels.

Miami's glow is on every horizon now.

He doesn't look, but he knows.

The sky is a langleic pinball machine he plays with his mind gone haywire he can't control complete with its bells and whistles and squeaks and now alas the emotional paranoia that preempts the feeling of something so good it's wrong so right the animate thing in here steps out for a sec as Too Much Acid, comes, in. Though Victor is an expert and a professional. At this acid thing. Trust me it slows talk to me. All structures and constructs obliterate and the physics of illusion and the illusion of physics as is what's real. Hear me. This is all in-ear whispers, Dad. I'm in here. I can hear. I can swim. Practically gilled over here, Dad.

"*Whisper...*"

The best way to deal with a deliquescing mind, Victor knows, is to play with the focus on a memory to keep what's left of the hyper devolving/evolving and parting of matter and mind intact, and so Victor relates to the explosion of universe an inch from his face, pulsating — the explosion of universe, not the face, or maybe the face, too, pulsates — how when Victor was a kid his dad had laughed at him once for hooking himself in the face that now gushes and pulses with the sky's in-motion constellations and the...the face...

'I was maybe seven or eight. It was Christmas. It was cold. For Christmas I'd gotten a new bike and a set of Rapala bass lures. A few mornings after Christmas morning I set out with my childhood neighborhood friend Alex, who'd also gotten a new bike. I remember his was a BMX and mine a Mongoose, both white. Alex'd also brought some new GI Joes he'd gotten. At that point in history I'd grown out of GI Joes. In fact I'd killed all mine the summer prior in the backyard with my M-16 BBgun. And but so Alex and I set out on our new bikes toward the lakes by our houses, in Kendall, Alex's pockets full of new GI Joes and mine of new Rapalas in their little plasticized cases. I remember the sky looked like gray matter. It was early. The air unclear. We arrived at the lake at the end of 135th Court and carried our bikes over the fence and then climbed the fence and walked to the lake. I began to fish, using my favorite-looking Rapala, a shallow-running yellow and gray glittery thing with two dangling treble hooks, and Alex began to play with his GI Joes in the make believe swamp at the lake's edge. About two casts in I got the Rapala stuck in some reeds. I began to yank to get it loose. I yanked and yanked. And yanked. Finally the thing loosed and came flying at me. I tried to duck but it caught me in the forehead. I thought it'd just gotten tangled in my hair or something, and so I tried to remove it, but it felt stuck. I took out my little Swiss Army pocket knife and cut the line and dropped the rod in the grass and walked over to Alex and said, Hey, can you help me with this? Alex took one look at me and started to scream. I mean really scream, shaking his hands and everything and jumping up and down. Alex had always been a floppy-haired sort of little pansy, but I hadn't expected him to react like this. I said, What? Alex just pointed at my face and screamed. So I went to the bike and carried it over the fence and then climbed the fence and rode home. The front door was locked, so I knocked, and my grandma opened the door and looked at me. She started to scream. I said, *Que?* She just screamed. This scared me, her screaming. As if I were suddenly scared for my own safety. As if I were really hurt, just I didn't feel hurt. My grandma screamed and in Spanish asked what happened. I said, *Yo no se*, then pushed past her and ran to the bathroom. When I saw my face in the mirror, *I* screamed. Shit looked fucking gruesome — blood running down my nose and both cheeks, two of the Rapala's treble hook hooks stuck to the skin on my forehead at the hairline, the fake glittery yellow fish's lip dangling between my eyes. Finally I stopped screaming at my own reflection, and with a cup I poured water on my forehead. It looked better without all the blood, and so I felt immediately better too. My grandma'd called my dad, and he came straight home from work. I half-expected him to scream, but dude just laughed. Dad called me a *comemierda*. He drove me to Baptist Hospital. On the way there we stopped at a red light and a car pulled up next to us. In the car was a little girl with blond hair in pigtails. She was in the backseat, behind the driver, playing with something I couldn't see, talking to it. When she looked over and saw my face she started to scream and shake her hands, not much different from Alex. Her toy was a little pink unicorn. I saw it fly out of her hands. She pointed at me and banged on the glass, shaking her hands and screaming. I heard her high screams clear through the two panes of glass between us. I smiled at her as we pulled off. But anyway I was the only person at the hospital with a Rapala stuck to his forehead. The operation was quick and painless. I had a big bandage on my forehead, where they'd had to shave a little patch of my hair, when the surgeon came at me with the Rapala and asked did I want it back.

You know what I told him?'

Who's Victor Llanez is half-floating, half-swimming, lalating at the echolaliaic sky who is also himself and no one and everyone he has ever known, trying hard to concentrate on his own from-nowhere words to keep the unruly mind in a straight line and not all hose-on-full-blast-sans-nozzle crazy like it wants to be. The happenings in Victor's sky and ocean are pretty much indescribable at this point, and loud, concert-loud, stadium-loud, and bright, like a bath like a shower of everything.

Brian swallows his panic. He won't give up until he finds Victor. He's got hang of *The Machine* now, running it a little faster than idle, scanning the ocean with the Q beam. He occasionally stops to scan more carefully and holler Victor's name. Brian knows Victor can swim like nothing you've ever seen, and in his heart he knows he's out here, swimming toward the glow. He fires another flare, "VICTOR!"

But for Victor the sun rises and falls on fast-forward. It starts like a dim orange glow to his right, reaches apically up, stops, swirls, fills the whole sky then falls to his right, still, but somehow west, somehow. The sun rises and falls several times, growing dimmer each time, and at night the sky is just a mess of tinselly lines. *Filigrees* is the word he can't find in his mind's ocean's mind.

Meanwhile Brian's panic keeps coming up like vomit. His heart pounds. His gut's and organs' glassware's shattered in there, where things hollow make a vacuum. Brian feels instantly bad and heartless for thinking, however briefly, about having to maybe cancel The Amazing Hair Drug Tour if Victor drowns man Victor's *not* going to drown man! Brian's voice is hoarse. He hollers Victor's name.

Victor is no longer in the Atlantic Ocean but in the amniotic fluid in his dead mother's womb where his mind is unborn. The sky is neither day nor night and glows inner worldly, the same color as the amniotic fluid, which is at best rainbow-colored and translucent and oily. He floats. He swims. He forgets his name. He is. He is not...in here. His mind simply refuses to work properly, no matter how hard he tries. It's like trying to grab air. It is nameless and spatio-temporally dislocated and for years now it's been pointless to even say this but yes it is socially unstructured and broken and mental blanks like balls go round and round in circles you can't catch to the point of almost psychic pain and for sure now he is *sine loco, anno, vel nomine.*

*

Who's Victor needs no longer to swim so he just floats. Things bump him from underneath. No need to worry about that. He's not in the ocean, it's only his mind. *Peaking Is An Understatement* is a statement that goes round and round and echoes in-head and *push* and *who* and the caress of smooth, wet, skin.

*

It's a few minutes before dawn, and Brian's nearly constant flaring and Q beaming has attracted more than one boat. Sportfishermen. A Mako and a Bayliner moor either of *The Bone Machine*'s sides somewhere off Government Cut. The sky is candy-colored, and the ocean is green, clear to the bottom. At several mph Brian tells the fishermen what happened, to all of them, all at once. One goateed fisherman wearing yellow Oakley's asks Brian why didn't he use the radio and Brian says he had no fucking idea there was even a fucking radio on the fucking boat and fuck that shit dude we have to find my friend NOW!

*

The sun is at its zenith. Who's Victor finds himself sitting out on some buoy somewhere out in the middle of the ocean with his feet in the water. He has no idea where he is or why he is out here. The blue-green water all around splashes, squeaks, clicks and just generally makes lots of spiracular noise. He sees dolphins, bottlenose dolphins. The ocean is maybe all dolphins. Like no water but just dolphins, writhing all over each other, flying out of themselves, twirling in the air, up where the sun is a nuclear mosh pit. He can hear the dog ear ring of the electromagnetic spectrum beyond the ultra and infra lengths of light. His ears sometimes bell. The sun gives Who's Victor retinal polka dots.

*

Standing on a dock at the US Coast Guard Station at Government Cut under the same ringing sun Brian calls Victor's dad Victor on a borrowed cellphone. Brian's hands shake and it's difficult to keep the tiny phone to the ear, which are both coated in sweat. Brian blathers to Victor's dad what happened and what's going on but neither of them can understand what he's saying.

"Calm down, son."

The deep thick Cuban-accented voice on the line jars Brian, and he and Victor Sr. are both silent, wondering is the line dead, each of them about to say: Hello?

*

Who's Victor's buoy is red, white, bobs with the sea. He watches clouds gather cerebrally, thankfully, blotting the punishing sun. He is nothing but thirst. And it rains. It really comes down. Who's Victor opens his mouth at the sky. It fills with water. He is able to take a few big swallows. His mind seems less unwell than simply unable to produce a coherent thought. Everything, including his arms, his body, is bathed in wet colors unnamed. Who's Victor knows nothing. Sounds are huge and faraway and deep inside the annular mind on a möbius loop of *where am I is the question is who am I is the question is where am I is...*

*

The search for Victor Llanez is on: boats, helicopters, the works. Brian refuses to eat or drink anything. He sits cross legged on the asphalt by the docks, in the rain, his cap on the floor next to him, his hair lank and wet and all over his hands, which hold his face.

*

Night falls. It's difficult to say why Who's Victor is back in the water, but he is back in the water, logging along on his back again in a direction only his bones know is shoreward. Who's Victor is pretty sure now his name is Maybe Victor, but exactly who is still a mystery. He seems to sleep unilaterally and swim automatically. He is bumped along from underneath. The caress of smooth wet skin. His sky is obscured by clouds that look like brains and suddenly it's dark with clear light and everything writhes and sounds are insane and impossible.

*

Hours pass. Maybe Victor's heels hit sand. He stands, chest-deep in the water. He turns around and sees the shore and lights and what looks like a sports bar. It says Aruba's. He walks toward it, plashing up onto the sand. The sea abandons his feet, and for a second he feels like sitting, but he's come over by thirst and staggers on wobbly sea legs.

Inside Aruba's this section of the place gets quiet. Maybe Victor is a sight, to say the least: some buzz cut dude, barefoot in jeans and a logoless gray T-shirt with a tit pocket, thoroughly wet, lashing a huge puddle of seawater around his feet on the floor, his face the face of a man who's shot out. He stands there not really looking around or anything. Lights whine. Vibrations a thing of the past. Totally used to them now. People stare and say nothing. Maybe Victor takes a few steps toward a table and grabs off it a clear pitcher of ice water. He slakes his thirst. Ice and water that doesn't get drunk fall all around and down his chest. People at the table move screechily back in their chairs wide-eyed and open-mouthed. Then Maybe Victor puts the empty pitcher back on the table and walks to the bar and sits on a stool.

The cold fresh water felt more like an ablution than anything else, he feels, on a sort of delay. But *refreshed* is not, the — word, exactly. He retrieves his sodden wallet and, resting his forearms on the bar, extracts a wet twenty. The bartender's a girl with piercings in her face and pink hair up at angles.

"Sir? You all right?"

"Fine," Maybe Victor says. "Just, uh, gimme whatever you got on tap. Bass or whatever." He pushes the twenty toward her on the bar, but it sticks crinkled to the lacquered wood, staying where it is.

The bartender goes and brings over a pint of Bass, not much of anything readable on her face. With a shiny black fingernail she peels the twenty off the bar and goes to the register.

Maybe Victor takes up the pint and drinks. It tastes like his first thirteen-year-old beer — hard and strong and fizzy, bitter. *Beautiful.* He looks up at the TV on mute. He ignores the little black boxes with words inside. On the screen is a familiar face, a face he knows he knows he knows but just can't place, the face of a man in a mortarboard, smiling hideously, and underneath the face it says: MISSING.

Acknowledgements

This book is a result of years of support from friends and family while I was away on a state-funded vacation. Special thanks go to Gabriel Morales, J.J. Colagrande, Janan Scott, Brandon Sparling, Oly, Tony & Maite, Dino Felipe, Otto von Shirach, Estibaliz Brooks, Maria De Arriba, Susan Valadez, Officer Jack Daniel Smith, Randy Young, Ricky Pollo, Mauricio Abascal, The Leon Family, The Caballero Family, Barbie Vasquez, Jennifer & Carlos Sardiñas, Jen Stark, Liz Tracy, Adam Gersten, Sam Borkson, Sabrina Morales, Hugo Montoya, Theresa San Juan, Deric Zacca, Ariana Fajardo Orshan, Jessenia Gonzalez, Javier Sasieta, Jennie Perri, Virginia Ansaldi, Emily Martinez, Paola Mojica, Frank Hernandez, Gerry Alvarez, Diego Machado, Nick Ruiz, and Rolando Martinez. I would also like to give another kind of special thanks to the State of Florida and Florida Department of Corrections for affording me the time to write (I am not being sarcastic in any way) and for providing me with a lifetime of material to work from. And most important, I thank my family: Mom, Dad, my sisters, Ana and Cary, and my niece, Lexy.

ABOUT AUTHOR

Luis Garcia was born and raised in Miami. He studied Fine Art at
Florida International University. Later, he spent 8-1/2 years in prison,
filling many, many pages, longhand. His work has appeared in literary
journals both in print and online. This is his first full-length publication.